THE WORLD OF THE BULL

whose inhabitants include Guero, the torero trainer who sends his pupils to the grave and his daughters onto the streets . . . Delia, a strange American heiress whom surgery has made even stranger . . . Armero, the blind ex-numero uno who owes his life to his unmentionable disease . . . Maria, a prostitute whose body may be in bed, but whose mind is on AT&T . . . Suitcase Morales, a thief who practices by stealing bras from his dancing partners . . . Doris, an apprentice nymphomaniac . . . "Nagadoches" North, a famous Negro black humorist . . .

What's a nice boy like Sol Feldman doing with these people? We wouldn't like to say. . . .

"The most bizarre cast of characters this side of MARAT/SADE . . . whacky, wonderful. . . . If you have a sense of humor, THE BOOTS OF THE VIRGIN is for you. If you haven't, stay away"

—Saturday Review

THE BOOTS
OF THE VIRGIN

EARL SHORRIS

A DELL BOOK

FOR *Grace Darling* AND FOR *Richard T. Kennedy*

Published by
DELL PUBLISHING CO., INC.
750 Third Avenue
New York, N.Y. 10017

Dell ® TM 681510, Dell Publishing Co., Inc.
Reprinted by arrangement with
Delacorte Press
New York, New York
Printed in U.S.A.
First Dell printing—October 1968

CONTENTS

The events described in this book are true.
The people and places are real.
Even the name of the author has not been
changed to protect the innocent.

Me cago en las botas de La Virgen.

A RELIGIOUS SAYING OF BULLFIGHTERS,
USED TO INDICATE ONE'S COURAGE AND
CONFIDENCE IN THE FACE OF DEATH.

1. SYPHILIS: THE GOOD DEATH

Before the Mexican could join El Sol de Michigan at his table, he had to remove the sandwich boards that hung on cracked leather straps from his bony shoulders. He stood the boards against the wall, and, feeling in his darkness with a cane, he found his way to the table. El Sol looked at the sign, preferring not to watch the blind man stumbling and hopping to his chair. He shook his head sadly over the words:

> ARMERO II
> FAMOUS BULLFIGHTER
> BLIND
> BY
> SYPHILIS
> YOUR
> CONTRIBUTION

El Sol had met his paretic companion on his very first day in Mexico, when he truly loved Ernest Hemingway and before he had taken the name El Sol. He had put a quarter in Armero's cup and Armero had thanked him, calling him Little Chief. During the next year and a half, while Sol Feldman had learned to speak Spanish and execute graceful passes with a bloodstained *capote* and a patched *muleta*, the two had become friends. Now they often drank together. Armero II paid his part of the check with stories of the great days of *tauromaquia*, telling of *faenas* and personalities that would never be equalled by the

modern practitioners of a sadly degenerated art. El
Sol gave the Mexican his complete attention, with the
exception of one small part of his consciousness which
he reserved for making certain he didn't get his glass
confused with Armero's.

It was cool in El Tapatio and damp. Skinny chickens and slabs of fat pork turned on a spit in the window, watched over by a legion of flies and a thin Mexican girl, who occasionally squeezed a piece of lime
over the chickens without looking up from her comic-
book novel. Several fans turned slowly. Water flowed
in the spitting trough beneath the bar. The bartender
and the three other customers in El Tapatio watched
a wrestling match on the television set, which was located high on the wall in a corner flanked by the head
of a Miura bull and a sword said to have been used by
Joselito himself. It was a Monday night in summer
and business was slow. Among the three customers
who watched the wrestling match was Bisco the picador, who waited for his fiancée, Maria Guadalupe,
to finish her work in the whorehouse so they could
have a few drinks together before they went to her
room for the night. Only on Sunday, Monday and
Tuesday nights did Bisco wait in El Tapatio for his
fiancée; on other nights he went to sleep when her
night of work was only beginning, awakening when
she returned with the morning paper open to the
stock-market page. El Sol lived next door to Maria
Guadalupe's room in the Hotel Xochimilco, across the
street from the bullring. He had often been awakened
by their bitter arguments over the market. Maria Guadalupe favored buying industrials on margin; Bisco,
who had grown up on a bankrupt *ejido,* preferred
commodities. They planned one day to open their own
whorehouse or brokerage and settle down to raise a
family.

When the wrestling match was over, Bisco would
probably join El Sol and Armero. He had once been

part of Manolete's *cuadrilla* and he liked to tell stories of the greatest of them all. Unfortunately, he had traveled with Manolete for only three months, which severely limited his fund of stories, especially in comparison with Armero, whose father had been on the same *cartel* with Belmonte, Joselito and Luis Freg, and who had himself fought *mano a mano* with Gaona, Rivera, Bienvenida and once with the great Manolete. He claimed to have known Ernest Hemingway and Sidney Franklin, the Jewish bullfighter from Brooklyn who was El Sol's inspiration.

This night the subject of Armero's conversation was death. An aspiring *banderillero*, whom they all knew, had fallen while boarding a boxcar and been run over. "You see," said Armero, "the dangers of travel. If a torero could stay in his own little homeland, he would avoid such dangers. Poor little Miguelito, he was such a coward he threw the sticks in like arrows from the greatest possible distance, and he is killed by a train. In the plaza he would have lived to be an old man; he was such a coward he could run faster on his two legs than the bull can run on four."

El Sol toyed with a hair that was dangling out of his nose. "Maestro, you should be more kind to the dead. What use is it to call him a coward now?"

"Gringo," Armero cursed, banging his white cane on the board floor, "you still think like a gringo. If you do not remember Miguelito as a coward, how can you remember Rivera as an artist? You see. You see."

The mention of sight by Armero always unnerved El Sol, who thought it unseemly for a blind man to speak of seeing. "I suppose I don't understand the Latin philosophy of death," he said.

"Oh, man," said Armero, "what are you talking about? Philosophy of death? There is only one thing to think about death: you should fear it. But you should only fear death for yourself. The death of others, eh, it's nothing, fate, the will of God, but your own death, that is something terrible. I know, because I have been many times at the gates of death. In Bogotá I was gored in the stomach, a mortal wound, five trajectories, seventy centimeters in all, and that was before antibiotics. Infection was already coming; I was losing so much blood. Death was already in the room with me, friend; I could see it on the faces of the doctors in the infirmary. And you know what I thought? Fuck, I thought, now I'm going to die and that will be the end, no more whores and no more Scotch whisky. The priest will give me the last rites and I'll go to heaven and live like a fucking Mason."

"What happened?"

Armero snorted. "What a question! I had to get well. I had three bottles of Scotch whisky and a little whore with the most beautiful ass in the Americas. She was the one, I think, who gave me this syphilis. How grateful I am to her! That little whore saved my life."

"By giving you syphilis?"

The weathered old head nodded in celebration of the remembered victory. From the bar Bisco shouted, "Olé! Armero! Olé!" The blind man turned his dark glasses toward the bar and shouted to Bisco to join them. "I'm coming right now," Bisco said, "because these bums wrestle like retired whores. I could beat them both with one hand in my pocket."

El Sol watched the picador ease himself off the barstool, thinking that Bisco was not exaggerating; he was big enough and strong enough to beat the two actor-wrestlers. He recalled a story about Bisco and Manolete: The picador had traveled with the great matador for several months; they had begun to like and understand each other, all was going well, until one afternoon in Caracas when Bisco was twice unseated by the same bull. It was Manolete's second animal of the afternoon, a big gray beast that took three perfect pics from Bisco without showing a sign that the head would fall enough for Manolete to find a place for his sword. The crowd was excited; it was an animal worthy of the great matador. The judges were impressed so by the strength of the animal they were going to allow the picadores one more chance at the hump of muscle. Manolete made elegant movements with the cape to keep the bull in the center of the ring while Bisco stood near the outside, urging his horse to its feet. Suddenly the bull broke away from the spell of the fluttering cape and charged Bisco. The picador, too angry or too proud to run for the protection of the *burladero*, doubled his fists and waited for the bull to gore him. Just before the horns reached him, the bull saw the *burladero* behind Bisco and slowed his charge to avoid running headlong into the thick wall of wood. It was all that Bisco needed. When the horns were only inches from his body, he stepped aside and threw a roundhouse right at the head of the bull. The punch landed just below and behind the bull's right horn. The animal took two more steps before it collapsed, skidding onto the sand. The crowd applauded, women threw their underwear at him, bags of wine fell at his feet, flowers sailed into the ring. Bisco was discharged from the *cuadrilla* of Sr. Rodriguez that night. The manager gave him a hundred pesos and a first-class ticket on a pig and sulphur boat which was sailing for Mexico that night by way of Buenos Aires, Patagonia, and West Coast ports. When he arrived in Mexico twenty-two days later, he was still a hero, but even his mother declined to embrace him.

Bisco nodded a greeting to El Sol and put his big hand on Armero's shoulder. "Maestro, what did you win?"

"Scotch whisky, butcher boy, and pretty whores."

"He says syphilis saved his life," El Sol explained.

"Oh, yes," said the picador; "he is a lucky man."

"You see, gringo, it is all in how you look at life. When you have fought as many bulls and been as close to death as I have, your eyes will be open, like mine."

El Sol became uncomfortable again at the allusion to sight. "I would rather die of a wound than of syphilis," he said.

"Ah," said Armero, raising a victorious finger, "but would you rather live or die?"

"Live."

"And would you rather live a long time or a short time?"

"A long time," El Sol answered.

Armero smiled. "And if you die from a wound, how do you die?"

"Quickly."

"But if you die from syphilis, how do you die?"

"Slowly, a little bit at a time."

"Then," said the blind man, "which is the good death?"

El Sol, stunned by the answer Armero's midwifery was about to elicit from him, muttered, "No. That's not right. You can't believe that."

"Well, friend," said Armero, "I can only tell you that it is a long time since the great Manolete had a drink of Scotch whisky."

Bisco laid a comforting hand on El Sol's arm, "You see, gringo, it is as it is said, 'There is no bad from which good does not come.'"

2. SUICIDE IS ALSO AN OPPORTUNITY

El Sol was lying in his bed, picking at the bedbugs that shared his room in the Hotel Xochimilco, when Suitcase Morales the thief knocked at the door. The moment Morales identified himself, El Sol leaped out of bed and began stuffing valuables into drawers and under his mattress. His phonograph, which was too large for either a drawer or the bed, he put into the bathroom behind the toilet. Morales knocked several times while he was getting his belongings to safety, but El Sol would not be harried into opening the door before he was ready. He would take no chances with a man who was said to practice his occupation by stealing strapless brassieres off his dancing partners.

"At last," said Morales when El Sol opened the door. "What are you afraid of? You don't think I would steal from you, a torero?"

"No," said El Sol, covering his fears with a polystyrene smile. "I was just straightening up the room, that's all." He shook hands with Morales. "It's good to see you, Suitcase."

"I have important news for you, matador; the impresario wants to see you."

El Sol, who had twice before been summoned by General Sanchez-Villa, once to be offered employment as the general's chauffeur and the second time to be offered a position as the first bilingual ticketseller in Mexico, was not unduly excited. "Do you know what he wants?" he said, without the lump in his throat that had occurred on Morales' previous visits.

"Yes," said Morales, "I know, I think. Taco Aguilar is on the *cartel* for Sunday, but he injured his testicles in a bedspring last night and he says he can't fight. He told My General he walks now like a turtle with two legs. I think you are going to be his replacement. You are to be in the main office of the plaza at eleven to sign the contracts."

El Sol was nearly overcome with excitement. He shook Morales' hand again, laughing, barely able to speak. "Thank you," he managed to say between gurgles of joy, "I'll be there."

"And thank you," said Morales, leaving in a hurry.

El Sol closed the door and began to dress. He looked at his watch to see how much time he had, but his wrist was bare. There was a white mark where the watch had been. "Son of a bitch!" he said, then thought, "But it's not important. I am going to fight in the plaza on Sunday. I am a torero, at last!"

It had been two full years since Sol Feldman first witnessed a bullfight and determined to be a killer of bulls. A fat boy who craved chopped liver and pastrami, he had lost fifty pounds to achieve the proper figure. He had also learned to speak Spanish with a near perfect accent. Whatever was necessary to become a torero, Sol was willing to do. He had quit his job with the Saginaw Hair Straightener Division of Michigan Colored Products Corporation the day after he saw two ears cut from an undersized but ferocious bull of the famous Tío Pedo herd. For two years he had lived off the insurance money left to him by his father, a steeplejack with an unexplainable passion for brown and white wingtip shoes with leather soles and heels. Now, with almost two thirds of the money gone, he was desperate for his chance to stand in the sand with a dead bull beside him and the crowd roaring for him alone. He also planned a career in films and an autobiography with pictures of his most exciting moments, though he was not sure that high-school dropouts were permitted to write autobiographies. He kept a diploma-by-mail matchbook cover in his wallet, just in case.

Even before seeing a bullfight, Sol Feldman had been obsessed with the idea of fame. It had first come to him, as well as he could remember, on the night of his Bar Mitzvah. His grandfather, Wellington Feldman (he was an English Jew), had been a wealthy merchant in those halcyon days prior to his attempt to corner the market on Tucker Automobile stock, and had given his grandson the best and biggest Bar Mitzvah ever seen in Saginaw. Eleven thousand people had attended the ceremony and reception, which were held simultaneously in the Saginaw Slaughterers' football stadium. Victoria Regina, Sol's grandmother, had made fifteen thousand hors d'oeuvres for the occasion, baking and freezing the first batch when Sol was four years old. It was as he stepped down from the platform that had been erected on the fifty-yard line near the East Stands that he realized what he had to do in life, for he had stepped up onto the platform with a face full of white-centered pimples and when he stepped down out of the spotlight his skin was as clear as Eisenhower's eyes.

Not for a moment did Sol delude himself into thinking it would be easy to become a torero. He had read Hemingway; he knew. There would be danger: dark-eyed women, jealous men with long sideburns, bulls that knew Latin, windy afternoons in strange plazas, Mexican lettuce. But he had resolved that he would be a torero and that nothing would keep him from glory. No sacrifice was too great. The sacrifices up to that time, however, had proved to be minor: he had not felt hot water for two years, he had lost much blood to the bedbugs, he had been robbed a hundred and eighteen times, and he had suffered eleven gorings and a skull fracture while caping half-breed bulls awaiting their turn at the local slaughterhouse.

Sol kissed his mezuzah for luck, then slipped on the shiny chartreuse shirt he liked to wear with his rust-colored trousers. In those clothes he felt less Jewish and more like a young Mexican torero. He made his own bed that morning, because he would be out when the maid came to his room, and he never allowed her into the room unless he was there, since her husband and oldest son were approximately his size. El Sol de Michigan whistled a *paso doble* on his way out, passing the rooms of Maria Guadalupe and the young torero, Veneno Hernandez. In the hotel lobby he said a cheerful good morning to the fat Indian woman who sat behind the desk. She had the American cigarette stamps pasted on her temples. He knew she was concentrating, waiting for the magic power to pass between the stamps and cure her headache, so he was not upset when she did not return his greeting.

After the adobe darkness of the Hotel Xochimilco, the summer sun was blinding. El Sol opened the pearl snap on his shirt pocket and took out his sunglasses. He blew the dust off them and slipped them on. Only then did he open his eyes to look around at the slow midmorning street. The old Plaza Freg looked good to him. He thought it was right that the walls should be losing their stucco and the wood around the gates and the ticket booths should need paint. "Tradition," he told himself, "is decrepit; that's what makes it wonderful." Hijo de Quien, his friend and a former *novillero* who now worked as caretaker of the plaza, was sitting in the shade near the entrance to the room in the plaza provided for him by the general. The caretaker looked up from the pushbroom he had been contemplating and waved to El Sol, "*Hola,* matador."

"What do you know?" answered El Sol.

"They say Taco ruined his eggs in a bedspring."

"What luck!"

"What luck for you," answered Hijo de Quien.

El Sol walked over to La Monumental to have an Orange Crush before going in to see General Sanchez-Villa. The restaurant smelled good in the morning; the open sewer that ran under it did not begin to foul the air until late afternoon. Consequencias the waitress smiled at Sol. "You better have steak and eggs, matador; you'll need your strength for Sunday."

"How do you know about Sunday?" said El Sol as he slid into a booth.

"Suitcase was here to sell the manager a watch, and he told us."

"That's my watch, I think. Ask the manager if it has my uncle's name on it, Bulova."

Consequencias went off to order the steak and eggs. Sol stared after her, watching her buttocks, which followed her for at least a foot. When he was a famous matador, he planned to take her to bed and find out if those buttocks really functioned as they were rumored to. Meanwhile, he had to plan his conversation with the general. How much money should he ask for? If Manolete and Dominguin and Ordonez had all made as much as fifty thousand dollars for a *corrida,* how much was El Sol de Michigan worth? He decided to demand a hundred dollars.

"The watch is yours," Consequencias said when she returned with the steak and eggs. "The manager says he paid forty pesos for it."

El Sol shrugged and reached into his pocket. "Here is the forty pesos. Bring my watch back."

She took the watch from her pocket and gave it to him. "Forty pesos is not much for such a watch," she said.

He nodded. "That's true; I've only worn it three years." The steak and eggs were cold and El Sol did not have much appetite. Besides, it was getting close to eleven and he didn't want to be late for his appointment. After only a few bites, he wiped his mouth with several tiny paper napkins and went to pay the check.

The manager congratulated him on finding his watch and getting his opportunity as a torero on the same day. "Yes," said El Sol, "good fortune is just a matter of luck."

The manager, who had never before graced El Sol's comments with so much as a nod of his head, let out a noisy sigh of appreciation, "Well said, matador. When Lala comes in this afternoon, I'll tell him and maybe he'll put it in his column." El Sol was pleased. In two years he had not once been mentioned by the bullfight critic. Even when his skull had been fractured, the Spaniard had not mentioned him by name. "Now," he thought, "my time is coming."

El Sol left the restaurant and crossed Railroad Track Street where the railroad tracks ran and entered the offices of General Sanchez-Villa. Suitcase Morales sat behind a desk in the outside room. "You are exactly on time," Morales greeted him. "My General will see you in a moment."

"Thank you," said El Sol. "If you don't mind, I'll just look around at some of the pictures." He had been in the office twice before to look at the hundreds of pictures of famous and not-so-famous, mostly dead bullfighters, that covered, overlapping, the outer-office walls. It was like visiting a museum or a tombstone to the art of *tauromaquia*. El Sol felt a chill as he let his eyes run over the faces of the great ones. The names were on his tongue. He could hear olés in the distance. "Some day my picture will be up there," he told Morales.

"Next to your friend Armero."

"I would be proud."

"You'd better be careful or you'll get the syphilis from your friend and they'll put your picture up in the Cruz Roja."

"I'm not afraid," said El Sol.

"You think only cowards get it?"

"You can only get it through sexual contact."

"My sister got it off a doorknob," said Morales.

El Sol looked at the Mexican and saw that he was not smiling. "Well," he said, "they say doorknobs are very dangerous."

Morales nodded. "You must know the same doctor."

El Sol was saved from more of the embarrassing conversation by the voice of the general. "Morales! Send in the gringo."

"Yes, My General," said Morales sweetly. He then glowered at El Sol. "Get in there. Hurry up."

The general sat behind a great mahogany desk, using three cushions to raise his fat little body to the height he thought suitable to his importance. His head was shiny bald. His eyes and his mustache sagged. Jeweled rings weighed down his tiny fingers. He toyed with an Arabian stiletto, which El Sol thought must be a letter opener. In the far corner of the office, a girl dressed in rouge and black mesh was sewing an obscene sampler.

"Good day, My General," said El Sol, slipping sideways into the room in deference to Morales and the general.

"So you want to be a torero," said the general in a voice that could only have come from a jukebox, for no human could make such a bass rumble.

"Yes, My General."

"You have studied?"

"Yes, My General."

"Tell me, gringo, do you think it is right that I should let a pig kill a bull in my plaza?"

"Yes, My General."

The general groaned. His eyes lost their focus for a moment. After clearing his throat and eyes, he said, "I have watched you practicing."

"I am flattered, My General."

A seven-foot-tall girl with six feet of blonde hair falling down her back crawled out from under the general's desk. She wore pink swaddling clothes. The girl and the general smiled at each other, but when she tried to kiss him, he threatened her with the stiletto and she retreated to a corner. The general turned back to El Sol. "You will appear in the Plaza Freg on Sunday, gringo. You have a Suit of Lights?"

"Yes, My General. Thank you, My General."

The general lit a long cigar and leaned back in his chair. "I have plans for you," he said. "If you show the same grace and intelligence in the plaza on Sunday as you do when you and the Mason pig Talclantlan are practicing, everything will be fine. Let me tell you, gringo, attendance is bad this season. The people want blood, death, and you will give it to them."

"My General, every torero kills his bulls."

"Cuckold, the gringos do not come all the way to Mexico to see the bulls die; they love the bulls, they roll in the droppings. What the gringos want is to see a man die, and you, gringo, are such a clumsy bastard —remember I have seen you practicing—that you will surely be killed. It will be the best thing for attendance. It will be in all the North American newspapers: 'GRINGO FROM MICHIGAN DIES IN PLAZA FREG.' What publicity! And for you, gringo, what an opportunity! It will be a suicide to be proud of."

"But, My General, how can you be sure I'll be killed?"

The general clapped his hands together with a clanking sound. "Ay," he said, looking woeful, "you see the risks of running a plaza? What can I do? Art is never sure. All I can do is to pray for you."

"Thank you, My General; I promise to do my best."

"Good, good," said the general. "Now, for the money: you will pay me five hundred American dollars. That is the price of the bull. You have your checkbook?"

"Yes, My General," said El Sol. "But, My General, I am resolved to become a torero. If the union hears that I paid you for the bull, I will never be able to fight a bull again."

"You will never fight a bull again, anyway," said the general, laughing. "But if you do not give me the five hundred American dollars, you will not fight in the Plaza Freg this Sunday."

El Sol took out his checkbook. "My General," he said while writing out the check, "if I am not killed on Sunday . . ."

"You will be gravely wounded, disfigured, perhaps crippled. I told you that art is unpredictable."

"But if I am not even wounded," El Sol said as he handed the check across the desk, "would you allow me to fight again in your plaza?"

The general looked at the check. "Gringo, if you leave the plaza on Sunday without a wound, it will be a miracle. Not only will I allow you to fight again in my plaza, I will build a shrine to you and every day of my life I will light a candle to you, because you will be chosen by God. But, gringo, God chooses very few. Take my advice, buy insurance, make a will."

El Sol smiled confidently. "There is no need for me to do that. I am one of the chosen people."

3. ART FROM THE BOWELS

Guero Talclantlan was born in a cave in Tabasco. He studied Spanish at a mission school, though his family spoke Tzotzil in the cave. In his early years, Guero practiced an eclectic religion, worshipping saints, snakes, jaguars, virgins, Christ and the moon. After his mother was eaten by a jaguar one moonlit night and the local priest refused to allow her into heaven because she had been eaten without the last rites, Guero left home to become a Mason. He traveled to Oaxaca, where he continued his education, studying anatomy in a butcher shop and surveying in a ditch. When he was seventeen years old, he attended a bullfight in Guadalajara, and decided that by combining his knowledge of bovine anatomy with his Indian courage he could become a great matador. Unfortunately, he was not brave and he had no luck in killing, due partly to his height—he was only sixty and a half inches tall. For some months he was distraught, even contemplating suicide, until he read a sign in a brothel in Vera Cruz which decided his career: "Those who can't, teach."

Guero became *peon de confianza* and maestro to several young toreros, all of whom were killed, according to Guero, before they were able to learn his method. In his middle years, he settled down in a border town to earn his living by teaching the art of *tauromaquia* to American aficionados. Among his best-known pupils were David Sloan, who had suffered an awful

goring in the ballpark in Cochino and left the bullring
to become a tenor castrati, and Mary "Bloody Mary"
Zinkthorne, who had been raped by a strangely horny
bull of the Matacoño herd. When Guero took on Sol
Feldman as a pupil, he was married and the father of
eight children, seven of which were still in diapers.
He lived with the children and his wife, Panzona, in a
one-and-a-half room house behind a curio shop on the
main street of the town. Panzona, though she was fre-
quently ill and unexplainably debilitated, was lo···d
deeply by her husband and children, who worried
about her constantly and were forever hoarding money to be used for Panzona's medical expenses.

Guero's first move after accepting Sol Feldman as
his pupil was to give the aspiring torero a new name.
"Sol," he said, "is no name for a great man. It's a name
for a man who runs a pawnshop." But Sol had protested; changing names, he believed, was basically
dishonest. So they had decided to keep his name, but
to Latinize it by pronouncing it as if it were the Spanish word for sun. Thus, Sol Feldman became El Sol,
The Sun. "My mother will be pleased," said El Sol.
"She always liked the name, Sol." Guero, too, was happy. He celebrated by making Panzona pregnant.

Every day but Sunday Guero and El Sol practiced
in the empty plaza. While El Sol practiced, Guero told
him the wisdom of the bullring. "There is no use to
run fast in practice; the bull will always have four legs
and you will always have two. The only one in the plaza without fear is the bull. To dominate the bull, you
must eat bull's testicles regularly. Courage is the con-
quest of fear. More wounds are given by hunger than
by the bulls. A poor teacher remains poor."

El Sol was touched by Guero's devotion. He knew
the Mexican had great faith in him because he refused
to accept payment for the lessons. "No, thank you,"
Guero always said when El Sol brought up the subject
of money, "when you are a great torero, I will take the

manager's share. Until then, we will invest together."
So every week when El Sol gave Guero the money to
rent the plaza for practicing, he felt guilty because the
little man would take not one cent more. And when
Guero bought things for him, El Sol suggested that he
take a commission. "Maestro," he would say, "you
went to all the trouble of buying this *muleta* for me.
You must take something for it, a commission, something." But Guero always declined, "A man does not
take the eyes of his child in payment for raising him."

As far as El Sol could tell, Guero and his family had
no regular income. They occasionally took some money from their oldest daughter, who was a prostitute,
which made El Sol feel even more guilty. "She is so
young," he often commented. But Guero explained to
him that it was best that way. "A girl can only be a
prostitute without fear before she begins to men-
struate." Sol was shocked, but that was in his first days
in Mexico, before he realized the poor have a wisdom
about life which no middle-class man can hope to truly understand.

The friendship between the two men was very
deep. They had experienced many things together;
they had suffered together. When El Sol was gored in
his first appearance in a *feria* celebrating El Día de los
Malcriados, it was Guero who had stood beside his
bed while the doctor cleaned out each trajectory and
sewed up the wound. And it was Guero who had
thought to comfort him after that first wound by telling him, "There is nothing to worry about, friend;
your bowels are not hurt. Remember, *tauromaquia* is
an art and art comes out of the bowels. You will fight
again, El Sol. Have confidence." The day after the fe-
ver finally went down, they took a bus to Tinnican, a
small village south of Oaxaca. The natives were celebrating the discovery of their city by the Spanish ex-
plorer, Cabeza de Caca. When El Sol was carried,
bleeding and unconscious, from the plaza, it was his

friend Guero who pinched together the flesh of his belly and kept his organs from spilling out, and it was Guero who directed the village doctor to wash his hands before he operated. When the drain was removed from the wound, they had gone to another *corrida* together. Every time he entered the plaza and was carried out, Guero was by his side, his friend. Even when El Sol's skull was fractured and he was unconscious for three weeks, Guero had come to the Clínica de Poco Socorro every day to slap his face and tweak his nose as the doctor had ordered.

Naturally, it was to Guero that El Sol went first with the good news of his coming debut in the Plaza Freg. Jesusita, Guero's oldest daughter was in the house, watching the children while her parents shopped in the city market. "Hello, handsome," she said to El Sol, speaking English. "Want to get laid?"

"You just stop that kind of talk," he answered, ducking under one of the cribs that was suspended from the ceiling as he entered the room.

"Don't come on queer," she said. "Let's make it."

El Sol shook a finger at her. "You keep that up and I'll turn you over my knee."

"You give me five dollars, honey, I'll show you better tricks than that."

"Jesusita, you're only eight years old."

She fluttered her eyelashes. "You don't want an old bag, do you?"

"When your father gets back, I'm going to tell him about you."

Jesusita went back to putting on her makeup. "Listen, honey," she said, thickening her mascara, "he don't pay, he don't get none, either."

El Sol looked for a place to sit while he waited for Guero. Because eleven people lived in the room, the only furnishings were beds. He cleared the pots and pans off the bed nearest the stove and pushed the babies over toward the wall. He found a dry spot and sat down. Jesusita watched him in her mirror. "It's cheaper here," she said; "you don't have to pay for the room."

"I thought you were supposed to be in school."

"Summer vacation. You don't notice outside, it's hot."

"No," he said, "I've been thinking about something else. I'm making my debut this Sunday in the Plaza Freg. I came over to tell your father about it."

Jesusita finished putting on her makeup and slipped the brushes and puffs into a clear plastic bag. "I got to be going, honey. Medical inspection today. I don't go, I lose my card." She started toward the door. "Hey, you watch the kids, huh?"

"Sure," he said.

She stopped in the doorway, holding aside the blanket that served as a door. Light poured into the room, sending the roaches into hiding.

"*Oye,* what does it mean, the English word, doomed?" she asked, speaking in Spanish.

He thought a moment, then answered her in Spanish, "It means you have a future."

"Yeah," she said, "wait till I get tits, I'll be in Hollywood." She let the blanket fall back as she left. The room became half dark again. He heard the roaches returning. All the babies began to cry.

El Sol sang to them. First, he sang Brahms' "Lullaby" and "Red River Valley." They continued to cry. Streams of tears and urine fell from the three suspended cradles. He sang Mexican songs: "You Don't Blow Now, Like a Woman," "Vengeance Is Love with a Knife in Your Heart," "Love Thief," and finally a *paso doble* he had learned from a Spanish bullfighter who was hospitalized with him at the Clínica de Poco Socorro, "A Swordthrust for My Love Is the Way of a Torero, My Heart." The crying continued until the three-year-old, the oldest of the remaining eight children, crawled out of his bed, struggling across the dirt floor on rickets-ridden legs, and whispered to El Sol. The torero shook his head, but did as the child suggested. He bounced up and down on the bed to make the springs squeak, and the little ones, as the child had told him, thought it was night and went immediately to sleep.

Half an hour later, Guero and Panzona returned. She balanced an enormous box of tortilla flour (the kind with the picture of the Quaker) on her head, carried a twenty-pound box of Carnation powdered milk in one hand and in the other two chickens that had died of natural causes the previous week. Guero carried a cracked egg in each hand. He had a limp *chile serrano* over his shoulder, which caused him to walk with a sideways motion to avoid kicking it. While they greeted each other, Panzona unloaded the groceries onto the bed where El Sol had been sitting. "Hurry up," Guero told her, "I'm tired of carrying these eggs."

"Pardon me," she begged, "but I have a pain in the place where my liver used to be."

"It is undoubtedly your spleen," Guero said, still frowning over the eggs. "I'll call the doctor to find out how much it costs to remove the spleen." He turned to El Sol, "The poor little woman, ever since we had her intestines removed she gets thinner and thinner. I thought it was the liver making her weak. A bad diagnosis. When the spleen is removed, ah, then she'll have her strength back."

El Sol, who admitted to ignorance of medical matters, said, "How can she live without her organs?"

"Injections, man! Injections! A Mason, a lodge brother, the pharmacist, you know him, Feo Xlatctanlt, he gives the finest injections in Mexico. And smooth, man. They call him 'Hands of Silk.'"

"My mother took a lot of Empirin," said El Sol, hoping to comfort his friend.

"Very good for headache, neuritis, neuralgia, but

those are diseases of old movie stars only. It is like your Bufferin; what need has Panzona for a relief that is gentle to the stomach when we had her stomach removed years ago, right after the fourth child was born? Believe me, man, for gentle relief injections are the best, but when you want relief fast, fast, fast, surgery is the only thing."

"He is right," said Panzona, who had collapsed on the floor. "And surgery has beneficial side-effects, not like pills. The pills have too many calories. But surgery, ahh. You know, Sr. El Sol, when I had my *vena cava* removed the hair fell off my legs."

El Sol, who had studied logic with Hedda Hopper, said, "But when you have removed all of your organs and veins, what will you do if you feel ill?"

Guero smiled his indulgence. "The nerves, the bones, friend, you think they are innocent?"

"Lobotomy," said El Sol.

"Amputation," said Guero.

Panzona struggled to her feet to take the eggs from her husband's hands. "What luck," she said, "to have two intelligent men talking about my health."

Guero took the *chile* off his shoulder and threw it on the bed, then he and El Sol went outside to talk. They squatted in the shade of the outhouse and smoked. El Sol told of his visit to General Sanchez-Villa. "You signed contracts?" Guero said.

"No."

"Very wise. Never put anything in writing: what is written may be erased, but a lie cannot be shot from the air."

"That must be an old Spanish saying."

Guero chewed a richly fertilized blade of grass. "No," he said, "I learned it from one of your indigenes."

They were quiet for a while, watching the amoebae multiply in a neighboring vegetable garden. El Sol broke the silence. "The general said I will be killed on Sunday."

"You do not expect to die?"

"Not so soon."

Guero scratched his crotch in contemplation. "It is a problem of anatomy, El Sol. The fear of death, you know, is located in the bowels, but art is also from the bowels. So you see the paradox: fear of death could be removed surgically, but it would destroy a man's outlet, he would become bottled up, bursting with the creative energies. There would be no solution for him, he would die of art poisoning. Believe me, friend, I have spent many hours thinking about this problem since I learned that art was a product of the bowels, and I know there is no solution. How I pity the constipated man!"

"When I am older," said El Sol, leaning back among the flies, "perhaps I will also be wise."

"One who makes a great deal of art need not be wise, son; he has the good fortune to be an empty man."

El Sol excused himself, smiling, and went into the outhouse.

4. A RAVE FOR FELLATIO

El Sol returned to his hotel late in the afternoon to find a note from Lala inviting him to visit the critic in his apartment that evening. "My God," El Sol said aloud, "I'm made." He showered, changed into his maroon slacks and green shirt, slipped on a pair of alligator *huaraches*, and went off to see the critic and columnist. On his way out, he met Maria Guadalupe, who was going to work. Since the whorehouse was in the direction of Lala's apartment, they walked together.

"You want to be *el número uno?*" she asked.

El Sol looked up at the evening sky and saw scenes of triumph faintly drawn in the clouds. "It's too much to hope for," he said.

She punched him in the shoulder. "There is always a *número uno*."

"I know that, Maria Guadalupe, but I don't know that I'll ever deserve it."

"Let me decide that. I say you can be *el número uno* tonight."

He blushed. "I'm sorry; I didn't understand you for a moment. No, I couldn't. I have an appointment with Lala."

"That queer? You would go with a queer over Maria Guadalupe! I spit on you." She spit on him, and turned away to cross to the other side of the street.

El Sol wiped his shoulder with his handkerchief, thinking he was lucky to be so much taller than Maria

Guadalupe. "Wait," he called to her. "I didn't mean that. I'm not going to see Lala for that."

She turned and spit at him again, hitting his left knee. "Liar," she said, "you think I don't know about Lala; he screws everybody."

"You're being unreasonable," he said, wiping at his knee.

"I hate queers. Don't you understand? Haven't you any sense of economics? Stupid, don't you ever think of the law of supply and demand? Don't you realize how they deflate the market? What I give is natural; I am an artist. And those stinking queers with their twisted ways, they ruin my market. Go with Lala, take up his ways, but I warn you, El Sol, if you do, you'll never be *el número uno.*"

"Crazy whore," he muttered, dismissing her, and headed for El Tapatio to have a drink to settle his nerves before going on to Lala's apartment.

Armero stood in front of the bar. On hearing El Sol's footsteps, he rattled his cup. "It's me," El Sol said. "Come inside, matador, I'll buy you a drink." Armero smiled and took his arm.

They drank tequila and talked of the coming *corrida.* Armero remembered his first time in a major plaza. He described the fear and the color, telling of the shock of sunlight in the first steps of the parade, and how it made him understand the opening movements of the bulls, allowing him to perfect his famous Suicide Pass. El Sol listened attentively, Armero had been *el número uno;* the paretic beggar had been carried on the shoulders of his admirers from every major plaza in the world. He knew the blind man could tell him much of how a bullfighter should conduct his life.

He touched the blind man's hand. "Matador, the general says I will die on Sunday. I'm afraid. What should I do about the fear?"

"Die. When you die, the fear dies."

"There is no other way?"

Armero shook his head. "You are too young for the syphilis; it is a reward for those who have had their times of fear."

"But you can conquer your fear."

"Fool," Armero laughed, "you talk like a fool. I, who was considered the bravest in my time, took my underwear secretly to old ladies after the fights so they could wash out the stains and no one would know. Conquer fear? Don't talk like a gringo. If you can control your fear, you will be lucky. You have been gored, right?"

"In every *corrida.*"

"You remember the horn, the weakness? You remember when you passed out, you thought you were dying? How can you now be without fear? When the shoulders drop and the animal charges and you feel it coming in the ground under your feet, you will shit a little. To shit is human, man; to shit without moving your feet is art. Control, boy, control. Let your bowels go. Concentrate on your feet."

"You never ran?"

"I never stepped back one inch."

"You're lucky to be alive."

"I thank God for my syphilis."

El Sol pitied him silently. He let the tears run for his friend. "You are never regretful?"

"Of the syphilis? Never. It is the best thing an artist can hope for in his old age. You'll see. When you are young, no matter how great you are, they will say you are only beginning to perfect your style. When you are older, they will only remember how much better you were when you were young. They want you to die so they can remember you and not be afraid you will deny their judgment the day after they give it. Only I cheated them. I give them nothing to remember, because I am alive and my syphilis makes me immune to them, even the critics."

"I'm going now to see Lala."

Armero rubbed the patches of stubble on his face, frowning. "He will do it to you," he said, already mourning El Sol's virginity.

"No."

"Ah," said Armero, "if only you had the syphilis."

"I'm not going to let him."

"You know, friend, when I first got the syphilis, before anyone knew, I asked my manager to get me a tour in a hurry. I wanted every city in Latin America and Spain. Twenty-three cities was all he could get me in that season. But it was enough. In every city, I called up the critics, all those queers, and I asked them to come to my rooms. I did it with all of them, just what they wanted." He suddenly lost his enthusiasm. "But the syphilis is a cheat. It's not a hundred percent. In that season, I did it with thirty-one critics and only twenty-five got the syphilis, and I think some of them had it before. It was a sad thing to find out. Since then, I have not been the same man. I became a cynic, El Sol, a doubter. Science, like God and art, is a fraud."

"Why are you telling me all this? I told you that I'm not going to do it with Lala."

The blind man drank the rest of his tequila and groped along the tabletop for his lime. "You want him to write about you? You want to be famous? Then you'll do what he wants."

"Did you do it to Lala?"

"No. I was before his time. But I have offered, El Sol; I am his whenever he wants me. I blow kisses to him whenever I hear his voice. And one day . . . You see, I remain loyal to my art."

The blind man reached for El Sol's hand, but the young bullfighter drew away, saying, "You are a good and true man, Armero."

"Yes, but my time is passed. Now I am limited to fighting a rear-guard action."

El Sol looked at his watch, which he thought of as new, and saw that it was time to visit Lala. He said goodbye to Armero and thanked him for his advice. As he walked out of the bar, he felt a touch of loneliness, wishing someone was with him to protect him from the critic; Guero was the wisest, Bisco the strongest, but Armero had the best weapon. He considered going back to ask the blind man to accompany him, but he was too much concerned with appearances to make his entrance with a blind beggar dressed in rags and sandwich boards. He wondered if he was being shallow, if an artist should not be above such things.

He walked a long time before he came to Lala's apartment, passing many handsomely colored neon signs and enticing storefronts. Shoeshine boys and taxi drivers called to him, causing him to feel a certain oneness with all men, for they were strangers, he knew, yet they spoke to him familiarly and with smiles. He gave pesos to all the shoeshine boys and begged the pardon of the taxi drivers, promising them all that he would return another time to avail himself of their services. The aunt of the dogcatcher, who ran a taco stand, begged him to dine with her, proferring a taco made of lean German shepherd, but he declined. "I have a Semitic distaste for that kind of meat," he said. "Perhaps you'll have terrier again soon, or bulldog." She told him she had some collie left, but it was stale. He thanked her for being so frank with him, glad that he was on such intimate terms with the people of the street.

Lala's apartment was near the old Cathedral of the Miracle of Repression, on the street where the people came annually from every part of Mexico to walk on their knees over piles of broken glass to show their love for The Church. Lala also loved The Church and went there daily, though El Sol had heard rumors that the critic loved priests more than The Church. El Sol

looked at the cathedral and shook his head. The idea
of Christ being the son of God and dying on the cross
had always seemed absurd to him: it made God out
such a bad father. He preferred either a nonanthropo-
morphic God or a better family man. Moses too was
suspect in his mind, because he knew orphans suffered
from psychological problems.

The decaying, almost new building in which Lala
lived had been designed by the famous Mexican ar-
chitect, Carlos Riley-Schultz. El Sol walked down the
steps to the marble entranceway, then rode the eleva-
tor up to the ground floor and entered the lobby. The
white plaster floor and parquet walls intimidated him
momentarily. Then, gathering his courage, he pulled
on the string marked "Lala," which served as a bell,
since the bell had been installed out of order.

"Come in, dear," the critic called. El Sol shuddered,
then went up the raffia stairs.

Lala stood beside the front window, which also
served as a door, holding it open carefully to avoid
being cut by the broken glass. He was dressed in an
orange cassock and a coonskin cap. Tiny bells, attached to his fingers and toes, were sounded by his
slightest movement. He ushered El Sol into the living
room through the toilet. They walked on a white rug.
"How do you like my antiques?" Lala asked, pointing
with an undulating hand to the purple walls.

"They must be very old," El Sol said of the whips,
chains, handcuffs and other devices that adorned the
walls.

"And Spanish, darling, every one of them was made
by loving Spanish hands."

"Instruments of torture, huh?"

"I prefer to think of them as religious relics. One of
the great traditions of The Church." Lala rolled his
eyes and sighed, "That was glory. One day we shall
have that glory again."

"My grandfather used to say that."

"He was a religious man?" Lala said, tinkling all over with delight.

"Yes, he was a paranoiac."

"Marvelous, marvelous," said Lala. "But now we must have our little vis-à-vis," he said, leading El Sol to an aluminum love seat. El Sol wondered if a vis-à-vis was better for his career than a tête-à-tête, but he said nothing, not wanting to appear stupid. He found the aluminum seat cold, but less uncomfortable than he had imagined. Lala did a pirouette before him, ringing all his bells at once. "How do you like my costume?" he whispered, beginning another spin.

"It's very colorful. I don't think I've ever seen anyone with so many bells on before."

"Provincial," said the critic, "so provincial. It's dreadful—or is it divine—that the young artist arrives with such terribly provincial ideas. It's trying, but in some ways pleasurable, to introduce them to more sophisticated ideas. I consider it an absolute challenge. And I'm very good at it, El Sol. Sometimes overnight I can change a young ruffian torero into a sophisticated man of his time. Magic, I have an absolute magic when it comes to transformations. You'll see."

El Sol nodded grimly. He tried not to look at Lala, prancing in his cassock, or to hear the constant bells; it made him nervously aware of the warnings of Armero and Maria Guadalupe. A premonition about the course of the visit came to him, and he wanted to get it over with before the premonition proved to be true and his career was ended right there on the aluminum love seat. "I think we should get to the interview," he said. "It's getting late and I'm in training; I have to get my sleep."

"Don't rush," said the critic; "it's so nice having you. Would you like me to play something for you with my bells?"

It was not without some effort that El Sol delivered

an affirmative smile. Lala returned the smile. "I'll play *Swan Lake* and dance it for you while I play." He began to leap about the room, waving his arms and wildly working his fingers and toes. El Sol was not sure that he was hearing *Swan Lake;* the bells seemed to him to be sounding something more like the opening theme of a Frankenstein movie. It amazed him that Lala, who was usually seen sipping exotic liqueurs in expensive cafés or strolling in the sun with his coat over his shoulders and his beret set elegantly on his balding head, could dance with so much energy and so little inhibition. He wondered if Lala was a very good dancer. He had only seen a ballet once before; a touring company had come to Ypsilanti to perform the *Nutcracker Suite* and his senior class had gone to the performance, borne there in yellow busses that smelled of carbon monoxide, Italian salami, butter and Evening in Paris perfume. It had not impressed him greatly. Perhaps, he thought, he had slept through the best parts.

Lala's dance went on for fifteen minutes before he gave a final fluttering tinkle and came to rest with his ankles crossed and one arm high in the air. He held the position for a moment, then bowed. "That's only the first act," he said. "Oh our next meeting, I'll do the second act. I would have done it for you this evening, but I've had a difficult day and I simply don't have the wherewithal to perform it properly. Alas."

El Sol didn't know whether he should applaud the performance; he decided to smile instead, remembering the Japanese maxim, "A smile always masks one's true feelings." It pleased Lala, who bowed again, then fell like a sweating feather onto the love seat. He put his hand on El Sol's knee. "It's a joy to dance for a handsome young man."

"I'm not handsome," said El Sol. "I have hair in my nose."

The critic leaned close to him. "Now, now, let us have no false modesty. Remember, it is by flaws that perfection is recognized."

"Yes, you're right. I hadn't thought of that."

Lala leaned back on the love seat and stretched out his feet. When he was in a position that he found comfortable, he began to lecture the young torero on the art of *tauromaquia*. He spoke of the dead and the great. His conversation was filled with quotes from the writings and sayings of Ava Gardner and Barnaby Conrad. Several times he was nearly in tears as he spoke of the great performances he had seen and the great lives he had come in contact with during his career as a critic and columnist. Near the end he spoke of the death of the art. "The classic form is gone," he said. "What has been done is all that can be done. *Tauromaquia* is dead. What we see now are only attempts at art. The form is used up. We do better to study the great matadores of the past than to watch those who fight today. I would rather count the hairs of Manolete's head than watch a present-day matador at his mediocre best; it is more exciting. For *tauromaquia* to become an art again, for it to be valid, there must be a new form. The bulls are different, death is different, we are different; a new form must be found for our time. Perhaps you will find it. You are young and beautiful, El Sol. Perhaps it is in you somewhere, buried deep in your secret heart. Who knows? I know only that you are beautiful. Kiss me."

"No."

"You must."

"I have a cold."

"No matter."

"And trenchmouth."

"I would consider it a gift. Kiss me now."

"I can't; it would be perverse."

"Ah," said Lala with a sneering smile unlike the smiling sneer he wore when watching the bullfights, "provincialism. I knew it. I could have told you the moment you walked in: lovely but provincial, sensitivities not fully activated. I know the syndrome; it's nothing new. A mark of failure, the lack of sophistication that keeps a young man from becoming a true artist. Of course, of course, why did I bother with a failure? You do know that a career is impossible for you?"

El Sol thought a moment, trying to gather all the variables of the situation and make a judgment of them. He stroked his cheeks, brushed at the hair in his nose with a knuckle, all the while knowing that Lala was watching him, waiting for his answer, holding his future in abeyance until he committed himself. At last, his thoughts clarified, ready for any response from the critic, El Sol said, "Uh uh."

"That's incredible!" said Lala. "You can't really mean to tell me that. What is the world coming to? I can't bear it. It's too much, just too much that an artist should say that to me. But I can help you, if you are artist enough to open your mind to the truth of the beauty of life. El Sol de Michigan, a new horizon is about to open before your provincial eyes."

"Uh huh."

"That's the spirit. Divine, just divine. Wait here for a moment. I'll bring us wine and beautiful cheeses to nibble on while I lead you into new worlds." He jumped up from the love seat and skipped out of the room to the kitchen. El Sol waited, considering whether he should take the opportunity to escape, but before he could act Lala returned, balancing wine glasses and a bottle with a four-foot-long neck on a tray laden with reeking, exotic cheeses and catalpa-meal crackers.

Lala impaled a piece of green and brown cheese on the small finger of his left hand and offered it to El Sol. "It's made from young tenors' semen, a mild aphrodisiac."

"Oh, I couldn't," said El Sol, who thought he was about to vomit, "I don't even smoke."

"Bitch," Lala said and gulped down the cheese himself. "But you will have one of these crackers and a glass of divine wine?"

"Whose semen is that wine made from?"

"Don't be foolish; you can't make wine out of semen," said Lala, tinkling his fingers disparagingly. He nibbled intensely at the cheese and catalpa-meal crackers. El Sol watched him without appetite. He drummed his fingers on the side of the love seat, waiting for something to happen, thinking he must remain alert to the tricks of the critic.

"I'll put you in my column," Lala said, blowing the cheese stench into El Sol's face. The drumming continued, but there was no answer. "I'll give you a magnificent review; you'll be famous overnight."

"If I have a good fight, I'll be famous."

Lala laughed. "Naïve, naïve. Bumpkin. You think anything depends on your performance? It is I who determine how good the performance is. Who in La Capital will know unless I tell them? Can they see you from Barcelona or Madrid? Lala is your judge, my dear, no one else. Even those who see you will wait until the morning and my review before they decide whether you are a talented *novillero* or a bumbling pig. I am your interpreter, and how I interpret you is based entirely on your pleasing me. You do it my way, or you are finished. Do you understand me? Finished."

"The general says I will die."

"There are worse things than death," Lala said. He put the tray on the floor, swallowed a last piece of cheese, then reached out for El Sol with excitedly ringing hands. "Kiss me now. Or I will teach you on Monday morning what is worse than death."

A stream of mucus, like a bullet, shot out of El Sol's nose and over Lala's shoulder, narrowly missing his cheek. The critic drew back, putting his arm before his face to defend himself. "Aaag," he said, "crude pig. It's always that way with your kind. Your nature fights me. But I'll win in the end."

El Sol sneezed, sending another mucus bullet in the critic's direction. Lala jumped off the seat and ran to a corner, holding both arms before his face. El Sol sneezed again. This time the mucus hit the floor at Lala's feet. "All right, pardner, dance," he said, and began firing volleys of mucus at the critic's feet.

"You'll suffer for this," Lala shouted, trying to be heard over his own tinkling and the thudding of the bullets.

El Sol increased the rapidity of his fire. "Art is invincible," he said.

"Whatever lives is corruptible," said the leaping man, almost breathless.

"Truth is beauty," answered El Sol.

"No, no. The truth will out!" shouted Lala.

El Sol held his fire for a moment, raising his head, taking careful aim. He let go a final shot, which grazed Lala's temple, knocking him unconscious. The ringing of the bells died away slowly. El Sol walked across the room, nostrils smoking, and looked down at the critic. "The fruit of evil," he said, shaking his head and holstering his artistic nature.

5. AN ENDEMIC DANCE

He lay in darkness, waiting for her. While he did not love her—no man, he thought, can have that feeling for a woman who aspires to promiscuity—in the way he wanted to love a woman, his feeling for her was beyond mere affection. She was beautiful to look at, kind, understanding of him. Often she could intuit what he could not say. They saw each other several times a week, and they always tried. He knew they would try again that night.

He passed the time in conversation with his friend, Sam, the leader of the roaches. Sam was, of course, unable to speak, but during the lonely nights when Sol had lain awake in his bed, waiting for sleep while he waited for fame, he and Sam had developed a method of communication: one rasp of Sam's jaws meant yes, two rasps, no; a clack was approval; and silence, disapproval. Lately, he and Sam had been experimenting with a square code, but the amount of rasping necessary to produce a single sentence was so wearing to the poor insect he was unable to properly chew his food for days afterward. They had been forced to abandon the project. It saddened Sol, because he thought there was much to be learned through communication with the roach world; on their dark side of life he expected they had learned to cope with many of the profound questions that still troubled humans. Despite their problems in communication, Sam had been able to explain to Sol some of the history of his species and many of their values. It was not easy for Sol to understand them, for their species was so much older than his and their traditions so much more complex. Their sense of history, too, confused him. Modern times for them began at the close of the last Ice Age, which made it difficult for him to convince Sam of the traditional aspects of bullfighting, a spectacle which Sam disapproved of, since roaches are historically nonviolent, and although omnivorous, do not kill even for food, preferring to eat that which has died by natural causes or been killed by some other creature. Sam's devotion to principles deeply impressed El Sol, who often asked his friend for advice and for support in adhering to his own principles.

Only on the subject of sex was Sam unable to help his human friend. He considered sex a useless activity that kept man from progressing into a more rational state. Sam blamed the entire reproductive cycle of mammals, including man, on an unfortunate mutation that had occurred during a period of great solar radiation in the old days. In all, he was not fond of mammals, who were, in his opinion, a violent and uncivilized collection of newcomers on their way to extinction. Whenever Sol attempted to argue the virtues of his own species, he was met with violent double raspings and determined silences.

It might have been the perfect friendship but for Sam's curiosity regarding human reproductive and pseudo (Sol believed in contraceptives) reproductive activities. Sam considered it absolutely protozoan—he made the metaphor by lying on his belly and waving his several legs in unison in the style of the paramecium. Nevertheless, he was always on hand to observe when Sol brought a girl to the room, adding his Victorian double raspings to the groans, sighs and giggles of Sol and his mistress. At various moments of excruciating ardor, Sol's peripheral vision had encountered Sam tiptoeing across the ceiling, perched on the edge of the dresser or the bedpost, and once, carried away by his curiosity, Sam had nearly been crushed by the act of love. Following that near catastrophe they had agreed to certain rules of observation: 1. Sam was to remain hidden until the act itself had begun, in order not to disturb the girl. 2. He was to double-rasp at low volume. 3. He was not allowed on the bed or the girl. 4. In return for those concessions on Sam's part, Sol was always to make love in darkness to avoid the anxiety caused to Sam by light, and he was to avoid girls who used too much perfume, which smelled entirely too much like insecticide for Sam's suspicious nature. Sam explained his paranoid view of the world by comparing his size and rationality to the size and irrationality of humans.

Sol reviewed the articles of their agreement. Sam answered with a series of single rasps and a final clack of approval. In darkness, the time passed like a stalled freight train at a busy intersection. Several times Sol thought of opening a conversation, but in his anxiety to have Miss Miller, he did not have the fortitude to endure the endless trial-and-error course. Instead, he told Sam stories of the suffering of the Jews in history, unaware that a distant relative of Sam's had lived in Hagar's house and that another had shared Moses' matzohs in the desert. Often Sam had tried to explain to his friend with the clumsy body and paucity of appendages that the roaches were the true historians. What they could have told Gibbon or Tacitus, how they could have helped Eisenhower, he would have said, had he not been limited to clacks and raspings.

"Remember the rules," Sol whispered to his friend when he heard Doris Miller scratching at the door. He pulled the light string, dimly vanquishing the darkness, and called out to her, "I'll be right there."

Doris was lovely. She had not been born lovely, nor had nature intended that appearance for her. She had been destined to be a girl with a sweet disposition

who cooked well and took up social work. Doris was a
miracle of modern cosmetology and parental devotion.
At the age of sixteen she had been lengthened to five
feet eight inches, an addition of eleven and a half
inches. The following year her ears had been trimmed
and her nose shortened and straightened in a festival
of plastic surgery. Her luxurious blonde hair had been
implanted one hair at a time, beginning after her
ninth birthday. Breasts had been installed before she
left home for college. The work had recently been
completed with the changing of her dull, lifeless
brown eyes to orbs of azure by an elderly ophthalmol-
ogist, who had spent his youth as a tattoo artist. The
slight impairment of her vision resulting from the
tattooing did not greatly disturb Doris, who claimed it
actually improved sunsets and gave life to black-and-
white art films. She considered it her crowning glory
and carried with her at all times the detailed stories of
the changeover that had appeared in the *Journal of
Plastic Ophthalmology* and *Tattooed Life*.

Though her parents had given generously of their
resources and love and she had suffered greatly to become lovely, much of life eluded Doris Miller. Three
years before she met El Sol, she had come to Mexico.
She had plunged into the culture with the courage
and delicacy of a conquistador, eating fresh vegeta-
bles, drinking tapwater, and buying tacos on the
street. But the revenge of Montezuma had been
wreaked upon her; in her absorption of the culture she
had learned to dance both the Mexican mambo and
the Aztec two-step.

After nearly four years of acculturation, she had become quite slim, though her bosom, which had been
grafted on so expertly, remained full and firm, with
polystyrene uprightness. She spoke Spanish with an
unexplainable Polish accent, covered her blonde hair
with a black rayon lace mantilla, and when not busy
with Aztec steps, she danced a plow-horse flamenco.

Doris had a permanent front-row seat on the shady side at the bullfights, which she adored. For a time she had contemplated becoming a lady torero, but the assimilation of one part of the culture made it impossible for her to take up the taurine aspect.

El Sol opened the door and drew her inside, clasping her to him for a moment then putting her off to arm's length and staring at her lovely, tattooed eyes. "You are lovely," he said. She smiled, her five-year-old teeth gleaming. "I do my best," she said. "For you."

"I like your eyes," he said.

"I often have the blues," she answered.

"Don't look at things that way."

"Do you think it's not in my nature?"

He embraced her and began whirling slowly toward the bed. When the distance seemed right, he kicked her feet out from under her. She fell onto the bed with great poise, letting out a musical grunt. "God, I love you," he whispered.

"Do you love little Doris, too?" she said, catching him in midair as he leaped toward her.

"Yes," he said, "oh, yes." He landed on her pneumatic chest, bounced lightly, then settled upon her, covering her face and neck with kisses.

"Then why did you bring up religion?" He continued his passionate kissing without a pause to answer. "I'm not interested in marriage, Solly." She breathed like a locomotive. He fell into the hollow of her neck, where he was momentarily overcome by her perfume. "What I want is a series of mad affairs now, because when I get married I'm going to devote myself to my husband and my children. I'm going to spend every spare minute in our station wagon."

Sol surfaced enough to ask, "Whose station wagon?"

"Never mind," she said. "Kiss me fiercely; I believe in promiscuity now."

"Yes, yes," said Sol the wanton, dreaming of Andalusian mountains and evangelistic rhythms. He wished for an old-fashioned girl who could undo her bodice and stand before him in her shift. Ripe breasts, he thought, are better than proud breasts. "Hunger goeth before pride," he said, with the taste of cashmere in his mouth.

He undressed her avidly. The scene had occurred so many times before, he knew her undergarments like the hairs in his nose; he could arrange them by touch, almost by instinct. She cooperated, lifting here and squirming there until she lay naked under him. "Careful," she said, "I'm still a virgin."

"Still?"

She nodded sadly. "El Sol, *toreador mia,* you know the problem."

"But not this time," he said, slipping out of his shorts. The sound of Sam, double-rasping on the ceiling, distracted him. He shook his fist at his friend, who lowered the volume of his rasping immediately. He smiled his thanks at Sam, then fell upon her breasts, kissing them everywhere but on the nipples, which were protected by clear plastic covers similar to the kind used on lampshades. "What about these?" he asked her, crinkling a piece of plastic in his fingers.

"All virgins have them," she said; "sophisticated men know that. If you were more worldly . . . But a girl must sacrifice something to be deflowered by an artist. Take me, *toreador,* I'm yours."

The matador, sighting on his target before plunging his sword into it, paused a moment to savor the pleasure of anticipation. It was too long. Acculturation struck. Doris grabbed her belly, threw her leg gracefully over his head, rolled away from him and ran to the toilet. "Again?" El Sol called to her as she was shutting the door. The answer came in the form of certain impolite sounds. He fell onto the bed and let out one painful sob. Sam descended from his vantage point on the ceiling and came to stand beside his friend. He nudged El Sol with a feeler. "Ah, Sam, my friend," the young matador said, "what do you think of that broad?"

Clack.

El Sol swatted at the roach, but Sam was too fast for him. He was halfway up the wall before El Sol's hand hit the bed. And there he stayed, loudly double-rasping at his friend's shamefully treacherous behavior. Sol stared at him, thinking, without finding comfort in the thought, of roaches he had stepped on during his short life. After a moment, he began to dress, muttering the trade names of insecticides under his breath. He considered a pogrom in the roach quarters behind the baseboard under the dresser. The thought of his power pleased and calmed him. He dressed slowly, careful about his appearance. A matador who fought in major *plazas* owed that much to his audience.

El Sol had finished dressing and was pacing up and back in front of his bed when Doris finally emerged. She was pale and weak. The very polystyrene of her breasts sagged with exhaustion. She was perhaps an inch shorter. Groaning, she collapsed on the bed. The matador looked at the decimated virgin, who gave no sign of life but an occasional shudder. "This is the worst," he said, "the absolute worst. It's been bad before, but I've never seen you like this. Doris, what's causing this?"

"Aztec gods."

"Don't be foolish."

She groaned, the sound of nails being wrenched out of boxwood. "I must suffer for my promiscuity, but I wanted promiscuity now, suffering later. The Aztec gods have turned it around on me. They hate me. They're anti-American."

"Be serious, Doris; you have a tropical disease, not a curse."

"If this isn't a curse . . . Anyway, I sent a specimen

to the Institute for Tropical Diseases. The report came back negative."

"All right, so it's psychosomatic."

"I've been analyzed." She groaned again, holding her belly.

He sat down beside her and stroked her head. She looked so pitiful to him, her bony chest with the ballooning breasts and her legs like discarded white angle irons. "Do you think it's all the gods or one god in particular?"

"I don't know. I talk to them a lot, but they never tell me their names. I think it's a lot of them, because they have different voices."

El Sol rubbed his chin, imitating Sam's favorite contemplative gesture, thinking how to approach the problem through logic. "When do they talk to you?"

"Only during prime time," she said. "They come in on my television set. Right in the middle of the best programs, the sound suddenly goes off and there's one of those gods' voices talking. I could get away from them if I'd do what they want me to, but I'm not going to become Richard Nixon's mistress and I wouldn't do those things they say he likes even if I was his mistress. Promiscuity is my credo, but that's disgusting. Those gods are filthy, just filthy. You just can't imagine how terrible it is to have a bunch of filthymouth gods after you."

"It's undignified."

"Oh, it's worse than that," she said; "it's tempting."

"You're right. Yes," he said. He wished he could confer with Sam about it. Sam could be objective, but what could he do? Here he was with a skinny, naked virgin with ballooning breasts and azure, tattooed eyes; he couldn't think of anything without the prospect of defloration obscuring the line of thought. "I wish I knew what to tell you, Doris, but I haven't had much experience with gods. My father and I didn't get on very well and I never met Ernest Hemingway. You should have told me about this before, then maybe we could have thought of an answer by now."

"I was afraid you'd think I was crazy, Solly, I really was. And I bet now you don't want to go to bed with me anymore. I bet you're afraid of the wrath of the gods."

"I am not."

"You would be if they came in on your television set."

"I don't have a television set."

"Well, where do you pray then?"

"I was a Christian Scientist until I made a girl pregnant and tried to get a Christian Science abortion. It was one of the great disillusionments of my life. I guess I had Margaret Sanger and Mary Baker Eddy mixed up in my mind, but at the time I was very depressed by it."

"I've always wanted to have an abortion," she said.

"I hear it hurts a lot."

She chewed a cuticle. Her eyes focused on something beyond the room. "Life, Solly; when you have an experience like that, you're involved in life. That's what I've wanted ever since I was a little girl, to get out of this humdrum and be alive. An abortion, that's life."

"Some girls die from it."

Her azure eyes shone now with excitement. "Solly, I'm not afraid of dying. I'm not any more afraid than you are. That's what I admire about you, Solly, how you can go in there in the ring with a bull and be so close to death." She clutched at her belly, drawing her knees up under her bosom, which blocked the route to her chin. "Oh, it hurts. The gods are torturing me. Whenever I get excited, they do it to me."

"Get rid of your television set," he advised.

"Please, Solly, lovers should never discuss politics or religion. Let's talk about you. I'm so pleased that you're going to fight in the Plaza Freg this Sunday. They've already put your name on one of the signs downtown: El Sol de Michigan, The Sun of Michigan. It sounds celestial."

"Solar."

"You're right, Solly. You know, you have a way with words."

"I gave a marvelous Bar Mitzvah speech. My mother wanted me to become a lawyer after she heard the speech. Maybe I'll be good in interviews."

"Oh, you will, you will," she said, taking his hand and touching it to her breast. "I have faith in you." He stroked her breast until she got another cramp and rolled away from him, cursing the gods.

They were quiet for a while. He listened for Sam, but heard nothing. He wondered if it was a sign of disapproval. Doris began to dress. Since her hips had vanished in the weight loss that accompanied acculturation, she had begun to hold up her stockings with long garters attached to her brassiere. El Sol was impressed with her ingenuity. "That's a great idea," he said, plucking a garter, which sounded a low E.

"Don't make fun of me," she said, pleading. "I'm just as frustrated as you are. A virgin's life is a lonely one."

He looked away from her, embarrassed, unable even to beg her pardon. "The impresario says I'm going to be killed on Sunday," he told her, hoping to win her sympathy and to escape from the subject of their frustration.

"Are you afraid?" she asked.

El Sol gathered himself into the stance of a brave man. "I shit in the boots of the Virgin," he said.

Doris hit him with her purse.

6. A DEATH-WIT

El Sol unpacked his capes, *muletas* and practice swords, preparing for his daily workout. Hijo de Quien, who had been in the plaza since early morning, working on the sand, sauntered over to the torero, dragging a rake behind him and holding a weed in his hand. He told El Sol the story of vegetation in the sand: "It is a very bad sign. Think of it, Solito, the plaza is enclosed by a high wall of seats. We do not put water on the ground except on the day of the *corrida;* if a bull or a horse shits, we shovel it away; so how can anything grow on the ground? There is only one thing to feed the plant, the blood of the bulls. It is a bad sign. We call this a bloodsucker plant, and whenever one is seen, there follows a grave wound or death for one of the bullfighters, and always a young one, who comes to town thinking he is *caca caliente,* you know. Be careful, friend, where this bloodsucker plant was growing was the territory of a bull that died for a long time this past Sunday. You remember? It was the second bull of the afternoon, Gringo Salazar's. He went in with the sword like a coward, into the side, the lungs, seven times before he could try a chop at the spinal cord. The sand was like mud from the pink blood that came out of the lungs. And there this plant was growing. A bad sign, matador, a bad sign."

"It's only natural," said El Sol, laughing. "Nature and a little luck for that plant, until you pulled it up. I don't believe in that stuff."

Hijo de Quien shook his head over the foolishness of the gringo. "No, man, you got to understand. Luck is luck. The seed of this plant could fall in some other part of the plaza and it wouldn't grow. You admit now that there is some luck involved?"

"Chance."

"Chance, luck, call it what you want, friend; you're in trouble. Luck for the plant means no luck for the torero."

"You really believe that?"

"Yes," said Hijo de Quien solemnly, "it is true, proved. They say there was one in Linares. They say Joselito saw one. I found one here in this plaza the week of Raton Ruiz's death."

"What can I do?" El Sol said, feeling a tremor in his bowels.

"Eat the plant, then you get its luck."

El Sol took the weed from the caretaker's hand. It was a flat, broad-leaf plant. The leaves were already turning brown from lack of water. "The roots, too?" he asked. Hijo de Quien nodded. El Sol shook most of the dirt off the roots, then rubbed the hairy stalk with his fingers until it was white. He took a deep breath, stuffed the whole plant into his mouth and began to chew. Never in his life had he encountered anything so awful. It was bitter and sandy. A rancid odor arose from the chewed leaves. He shivered. His eyes watered, but he continued to chew the leaves. When he bit into the root, another flavor, that of something dead and rotten, spilled into his mouth. He spit out the weed before he was compelled to vomit.

The chewed plant lay in a pile on the sand. It had turned red while he chewed it. "You see," said the caretaker, "you should have eaten it. I told you."

While they were looking down at the plant, which was rapidly drying up in the sun and the absorbent sand, Guero Talclantlan arrived. He joined El Sol and the caretaker in looking at the plant. "A bloodsucker?"

he said. They nodded. "Thanks to God that you didn't eat it. To eat that plant is to die for sure the next time you face a bull."

Hijo de Quien stamped his foot angrily. "You know that the bloodsucker means a grave wound or death unless you eat the plant to get its luck."

Guero laughed. "You think anyone believes that superstition? The scientific truth is that, if you eat the plant, you die."

"What if you only eat part of the plant, like I did?" El Sol asked.

The caretaker and the trainer lowered their heads and stared at the ground. Neither of them spoke. "No chance?" said El Sol. Guero smiled. "Who knows? I would advise you not to eat the day of the *corrida*. With modern surgery and the miracle drugs . . . If you don't eat, the operation will be easier. You know that from the other times."

"He is not a bleeder?" the caretaker asked.

"He takes wounds like the bull takes *banderillas*," Guero answered. "He should be dead three times now, but here he is. He has the luck of a martyred saint."

"You mean the martyred saints have given me luck," said El Sol.

"We'll see," Guero answered. "We'll see. Right now, let's practice with the cape. You did your warmup exercises?"

"I'll start now," said El Sol, beginning to run backwards. He made two laps around the outside of the ring and was starting the third and final lap of his exercise when Delia Monroe and a tall Negro stepped through the gate of *cuadrillas*. Delia, the daughter of the president of the Moloch Corporation, wore a sprinkling of diamonds in her hair and dragged a mink coat behind her in the dust. She had thick legs and tightly packed buttocks, but her shoulders were thin, and she appeared to have no breasts at all. There was a rumor that she was actually two girls skillfully

joined after the lower half of the real Delia Monroe
had been lost in an unfortunate automobile accident.
The rumors also told of a poor Polish girl in Chicago
who had traded her lower half for Delia's remains and
a trust fund. El Sol did not believe the rumors, although he hoped someday to encounter Delia in the
nude so he could inspect her waist for marks of plastic
surgery. He liked her, particularly her face, which was
bony in the haughty way of fashion models. There
were little rich-girl lines around her mouth. Her skin
was deeply tanned. Blonde streaks, made by the sun
and glorified by her hairdresser, ran through her black
hair, alternating with the diamonds.

Delia introduced her companion to El Sol, who was
breathing heavily and beginning to sweat: "This is
Nagadoches North—I'm sure you've heard of him—
the famous writer. He wants to do an interview with
you."

"Pleased to meet you, Mr. North." They shook
hands. "I'm afraid I don't read much since I got in
training, only a little Hemingway now and then. What
kind of writing do you do? I'd like to get one of your
writings to read."

"I'm a humorist, a black humorist."

"Yes," said El Sol, "I see."

North laughed. "No, not that, boy; it's a special kind
of humor."

"Well, even if you are colored, I don't think this is
the right time to be telling jokes on colored people. I
support Martin Luther King."

North laughed again. "I'll show you what I mean,
son. Feed me a line."

El Sol thought for a moment, then he said, "Who
was that lady I saw you with last night?"

"That was no lady," North answered; "that was your
mother, fucker."

"I'd rather you didn't talk that way about my mother, mister, or I'll hit you right in the mouth. Martin

Luther King notwithstanding, of course."

"Just calm down, boy. A black humorist is some-body who sees terrible things like you see funny things. When I write I don't mean to entertain, I mean to hurt. I give pain, see. I know how to hit below the belt, and that's where I like to get my readers. While they're laughing, I kick 'em right in the nuts. Take your story, for example. The rumor has it that you're a cinch to get killed this Sunday. Now, I think that's a scream. Hah hah, got it? I interview you here and then you die on Sunday. Your whole sordid little life gets wrapped up in less than a week. The human condition, get it? It means something about the absurd state in which we live. How can we survive if we don't laugh? You see, if you die in the end no matter what, life has got to be a joke and death has to be the funniest thing of all. That's why you're such a scream. Now, do you understand?"

El Sol looked at North, then at Delia, then back to North again. They were both laughing. North was doubling over, slapping his knee. "I don't like your attitude," El Sol said to the Negro.

"But you'll do the interview?" North said.

"Do it!" Delia shouted. "Do it, do it doit!" She jumped up and down, chanting, "Doit doit doit, doit doit doit."

El Sol looked at her blouse to see if there was any sign of a bosom bouncing under the silk, but he couldn't pin down any independent movement. "Okay," he said, "if you'll stop that jumping up and down; it makes me nervous."

"All right, boy," said North, taking a ballpoint pen in the shape of a thumb out of his breast pocket and beginning to write on the stenographer's pad he had been holding in his left hand. "Your name is El Sal."

"No. El Sol. S-A-L means 'salt' in Spanish. My name is S-O-L; that means 'sun.' "

"Oh, that's heavenly, baby."

Delia said, "Celestial." El Sol did not speak.

"You think you'll get to heaven on a bull's horn?" North said. Without waiting for a reply, he went on: "You came here for a taste of fame, didn't you? How absurd! There is no immortality, boy. This is it. That's the great gag. You want to make it with future generations and you'll never know—that is, if there are any future generations. I mean, you have to think of the bomb. It has to be in your consciousness all the time, like sex, you know. Man, you are so pitifully hilarious. Death is going to come over you like laughing gas. There you'll be, all decked out in that shiny shroud, choking your balls and everything, your arms weighted down with the death wish, twenty-five pounds of death wish—I better make a note of that one—and the crowd will be yelling for you to get dead. Wow! The humor of it is too much. In your little quest for immortality, a bull shoves a phallic horn into you and out you go on a fag note. Barrooop! I wonder if it's even existential. Yeah, suicide always is. You can't be God, so zap! and you're out. Oh, baby, do I understand you! You're so clear, like transparent. You push me to burlesque, you know."

"Aren't you going to ask me any questions?"

"Good boy," said North, without looking up from his notepad. "Yes, baby, yes, I'm going to ask you some questions. I want to get your speech patterns. I'd ask you some other things, too, like how you feel about death, but I know what you'll say. You don't expect to die. You really do expect to become God as represented in your fantasies by the hero. Beatification, deification by applause. Seeing your name in the paper is like seeing it in the Bible. Your name on the poster is like a crucifix in a church. You see, the whole construct is clear. You've made an absurd structure, one of the most perfect I've ever seen. I have to hand it to you, you are probably the most heuristic cat there ever was; your existence forces me to look further into the nature of absurd acts and the humor of them. It's the role of the true intellectual in our time, you know, to be prompted to laughter by what was once considered the tragedy of man. Dig? In a time when we can't even hope to endure, let alone survive, to find a man who expects to become God in a Spanish clown suit is really a find. You're too beautiful, baby, too beautiful."

Guero came over to find out why El Sol had stopped exercising. Hijo de Quien followed him. When they joined the group, North asked, "Who are these two?"

"My manager and the caretaker of the plaza," El Sol answered, pointing to each one as he described him.

"The Apostles!" North shouted, and began to giggle. Barely able to speak because of the giggling, he said, "Peter turns out to be a hotshot Mexican publicity man, and maybe Judas is the skulking caretaker of a bullring. The never-ending cycle of absurdity. There will always be a two-bit messiah. Hey, are you Catholic?"

"Jewish," El Sol answered.

North leaped into the air, then fell onto the sand. He lay on his belly, kicking his feet and pounding the sand, laughing. Delia took his arm and tried to lift him to his feet. Guero and Hijo de Quien helped her. At one point, halfway up, North lost his breath and began a rheumy choking. Hijo de Quien pounded his back with a fierceness he reserved for strangers. When North had regained his composure, he told El Sol, "You're a dream. Proof, boy, proof. Oh, daddy, a Jewish bullfighter with a death wish and a God dream. You are the mute nymphomaniacal liquor-store-owner chick of literature. Do you know what it means to be Jewish?"

"Jews have suffered a lot," said El Sol.

North suddenly became serious. "Oh, now, baby,

come off it. How can you compare the suffering of the Jews to what the Negro has suffered in America? And don't give me that six-million-in-the-ovens shit, man. Because that just doesn't compare to what we've known. Do you know my father was castrated by some fucking lousy white man?"

"I'm sorry," said El Sol: "It must have been a terrible experience for you, too."

"I wasn't born till two years later, but it's terrible just knowing it. The deep psychological scars."

"Then he wasn't really your father."

Nagadoches looked at El Sol for a long time before he spoke. "Don't patronize me, whitey. Just watch out or I'll show you a little black power that'll make you sorry you were ever born white."

"C'mon, Nag," said Delia, putting her hand on his arm, "let's finish the interview."

North took up his pen and pad again. He was covered with red dust. Tears made streaks in the dust on his cheeks. His lips trembled. "I'm looking forward to Sunday, Jewboy, when Mr. Goldberg, the beast of Harlem, gets his. You think I don't know about Jews? Well, baby, I do. You got all the money from robbing the poor. I know that. I know how you laugh in your temples where you count your money. We all know about you. Black liberals aren't stupid, you know."

"Nag, stop it!" Delia said.

"It's all right," El Sol told her. "In just about one minute I'm going to knock his teeth down his throat. That'll shut him up."

"So, Miss Ann and Mister Charlie are forming a little alliance," North said. "I expected it. The Jews and the capitalists, greed meets money. Why don't you screw each other? That would be just perfect. Give him a little heaven before he dies. Play Magdalene. That'll make it even funnier. He thinks he's Bogart and he's really Lou Costello. The little Christ dies in his little glittering suit. He thinks he's God. Tell it to the worms, Sunny, tell it to the worms. Baby, they'll really tickle you. Hah, hah, you dig?

"And you," he turned to Delia, "go ahead, fuck him. Go ahead."

She stepped away from Nagadoches and toward El Sol. With a half smile, she whispered, "I will. Yes, I will. If you want to, matador. Do you?"

"You bet," said El Sol.

"Be at my place at nine. There's a party first."

"Yes," he said, beginning to run backwards.

7. RACIST GENITALIA

Sam and El Sol began to talk as soon as it became dark enough for Sam to emerge from his hiding place. El Sol was in a foul mood, due in part to his unpleasant conversation with Nagadoches North earlier in the day. He told Sam about the black black humorist first, then confessed that he was also troubled by the constant predictions of his death. He was angry, too, at the cleaning woman. While he had been practicing *veronicas* and *naturales* in the plaza, she had entered his room to make the bed and, finding nothing else to steal, had made off with his toilet. "I don't know if it's worth all this to be an artist," he told Sam, "I just don't know."

He and the cockroach conversed for two hours. Although only El Sol could talk, it was he who actually did the listening. He needed advice and support, and Sam was the only one he could trust to speak to him objectively. Sam had difficulty understanding El Sol's fear of death. Roaches, he explained, were able to pass on all knowledge genetically. They were thus not individual creatures, but a succession of bodies in which knowledge grew without interruption. Death was of little consequence to them since life was thought to be a series of endless transitions, like the points on the straight line of Euclidian geometry.

Art was equally incomprehensible to Sam. From what the roaches had been able to observe of humans, he told Sol, art was a result of the frenetic nature of their lives, a direct result of their awareness of mortality. The artist seeks immortality by making art and the audience seeks a heightening and an explanation of a very brief life through observing art. There was also a sexual connotation to the whole matter, as far as the roaches could tell, but that was too alien for them to try to understand. The relation of sex to death, like war between nations, baffled them. There was a limit, he said, to the degree of irrationality a rational animal could comprehend.

"What if I stepped on you? Would you care?" El Sol asked.

Double rasp.

"You wouldn't care, because you have nothing to live for?"

Double rasp.

"Because your life would not end, only your body?"

Rasp.

"Okay," said El Sol, raising his foot over Sam, "let's see if you're telling the truth. Goodbye, Sam."

Double rasp. Double rasp. Sam streaked away to safety under the dresser. After a moment or two near the wall, he inched forward to where El Sol could see him.

El Sol laughed, but it was not a happy sound; there was vitriol in it. "So," he said, "all this time I've been throwing rotten food under the dresser for you and your relatives, I've been supporting an artist's colony."

Double rasp.

"Crap. I bet this summer you'll be out caping June bugs."

Double rasp.

"Sam, I'm sick and tired of your cockroach superiority. Face up to it, Sam, you're no better than a lot of human beings I know."

2

On his way to the party El Sol stopped at El Tapatio for a snack and a beer. Delia had not said what kind of party she was giving, and he made it his business never to drink on an empty stomach. He found Bisco and Armero at a table in the back. They were arguing.

"Good to see you," Armero said. "We were just talking about you. They are giving bets around the plaza on the *corrida* this Sunday. The general is giving three-to-one that you will be killed by the first bull. I want to bet with him, but Bisco is saying that I should wait until the bulls arrive and the *sorteo* is over. He says that if you get one with open horns, the general should give at least five-to-one."

"I don't intend to be killed."

"The horse's mouth," said Armero.

"Hah!" Bisco shouted. "The road to the cemetery is paved with such intentions. Besides, Hijo de Quien himself told me that when El Sol ate the bloodsucker it turned red in his mouth. A grave wound is certain. Then infection, and *adiós*. Or maybe they can't stop the bleeding. Maybe he's wounded in the leg, they amputate and then, *adiós*. Five-to-one is even robbery. Armero, friend, you have to beg very hard for your money. Why should you give such a gift to the general? He has plenty already."

"What does a picador know?" the blind man said. "A picador learns his trade by butchering pigs, a matador is an artist. Can a butcher judge the work of a surgeon? For a picador to judge a matador is like a dog trying to fuck a horse."

Bisco asked coolly, "You have seen him fight, maestro?"

"I am not as blind as your horse, bastard."

"Hey, friends," El Sol said, "could this wait till another time when I'm not around? I really don't like hearing it. Besides, I want to eat, and it turns my stomach. Do either of you want any *carnitas?* I'm buying."

"Buy them for your friend," Bisco said; "he can't see the flyspecks and he likes the taste."

"A small order," said Armero. "And thanks, matador."

El Sol left the table and went to the front of the bar, where the small pieces of pork were cooking on a spit. The girl who brushed the flies away smiled at him. "*Carnitas, señor? Pollo asado? Costillas?*" He looked at the food, greasy and brown, and at the dirty blue tile around the spit. A grinning, fat blue fly emerged from the carcass of one of the chickens turning on a spit next to the *carnitas.* The fly moved over to one of the *carnitas* in an act of cross-pollination. El Sol watched it walk around the piece of pork, moving at the same speed as the pork, keeping its shiny body and transparent wings turned away from the heat of the charcoal in the stone pit. The girl swatted lazily at the fly, which moved off the *carnitas* and back to the chicken. Other flies gathered on the limes that lay in a bowl next to the pit. The window in front of the pit was dotted with flies and droppings. "It looks delicious," said El Sol. "I'll have two small orders of *carnitas.*" The girl put down her comic-book novel and lifted one of the spits off the fire. She scraped the *carnitas* onto two plates, then added some French-fried potatoes that had been simmering in a pot of grease. "Fifteen pesos," she said, pushing the plates toward El Sol. "Tortillas," he said. She passed him a bundle wrapped in a napkin. He gave her twenty pesos. While he waited for her to separate five pesos from a wad of bills she fished out of the pocket of her apron, he occupied himself with waving flies away from the plates. "Enjoy them," she said when she gave him the money. "They are of a very delicate flavor."

Armero ate his meal before El Sol had finished a single piece of pork. "How long since you ate?" Bisco asked the blind man.

"Two days, three days, I don't know. I was saving my money to make the bet with the general. You see, I need five hundred pesos to buy an animal to help me get around. A man I know, a former doctor, says he is training cats to act like seeing-eye dogs. But the cats are much cheaper and also they don't eat so much."

"I heard of a blind man in Mazatlan," said Bisco, "who has an iguana on a string that leads him everywhere. An iguana is cheaper even than a cat. It won't scratch you, either."

El Sol laughed. "Bisco, how could a man ever trust a lizard?"

"Don't be that way," Armero said. "In this life we trust worse things than lizards. Those who can see, for example, trust their eyes, yet we all know that appearances can be deceiving. The cuckold sees faithfulness in the eyes of his wife."

"I'll remember that," said El Sol. He paused to swallow a piece of potato that had been greased for the action. "Armero, you're a wise man. You've been in all the great plazas, you've fought the best bulls, Miuras, Matacoños, Tío Pedos, Santa Condenadas—tell me what you think my chances are on Sunday."

Without hesitation the blind man answered, "I have great faith in modern surgery. You will live, friend. It would be the most incredible of accidents if you died. There is almost no possibility of a fatal wound these days. The general is only giving the bets to draw a crowd. No, man, I have no doubt they will take you from the plaza in an ambulance, but death, I don't see it."

"Sure he doesn't see it," Bisco said; "he is blind. But I am cross-eyed. I see it twice."

3

Bisco and Armero had also been invited to Delia's party. Bisco had to stop by the whorehouse to pick up Maria Guadalupe on the way. Armero and El Sol accompanied him. "Maria is working," Bisco explained. "She's going to be in some kind of show first, then she'll fuck whoever wants to. Delia always hires her for parties, because she likes everybody to have a good time."

"Since you are a guest," Armero said, "you can also fuck Maria."

"No. Delia says I can't take up Maria's time, and Maria says she won't let you touch her. Those are the rules."

Armero nodded, "Of course. You would expect that of a picador's whore and the daughter of a gringo millionaire. The whore has no taste and the gringa has no idea how many lives have been saved by the syphilis. Disgusting business. I only hope she's well paid for it."

"She gets one share of AT&T, except when she puts on a show, then she gets two shares."

They stopped for a traffic light. Armero tapped his cane on the curb, feeling the distance to the street. "This AT&T, it's a good deal?"

"I think so, maestro. The yield is not terribly good, but as a gift, it's the perfect stock. Dividends are regular, and the general trend of the stock has been up for many years now. It promises a decent long-term gain, the company being so stable. But I personally prefer to deal with commodities, where the gains are quick. Besides, I was born in the country, I understand wheat and corn and cotton. What do I know about communications or aerospace? That Maria, though, she believes in common stock. She says that Christ, cunt and common stock are the only things a woman can have faith in. And who am I to argue? The woman has lived a fine life and she has a secure future; which of us can say the same?"

"I see," said Armero as they crossed the street. On the opposite corner a legless beggar waited for them, balanced on his head on a roller skate, his stumps waving in the air. "One peso, please," he said to El Sol, "for an artist."

The torero looked down at the man's upside-down head, peering into his nose. "You're not an artist," he said; "you're a beggar."

The legless man shook one of his stumps in El Sol's face. "Don't call me a beggar. Can't you tell the difference between a beggar and an artist? A beggar would be sitting on his stumps. An artist puts his stumps in the face of the crowd and gets paid for it. Don't you see that? Presenting the stumps is my art and standing on my head this way on a roller skate is my craft."

"He does it very well," Bisco said.

"I have a unique view of the world," the beggar told them.

El Sol gave him fifty centavos and the beggar rolled off down the street. "Aren't you even going to thank me?" El Sol called after the beggar. Without slowing down, the beggar called back, "An artist does not thank his audience for money. The money is the way they thank him for being an artist." He smiled, though it looked strangely like a frown, and shouted to them, "You're welcome. You're welcome."

A small boy with an open cigar box full of chewing gum approached them. "Chiclets," he advertised, "aphrodisiac chiclets."

El Sol grabbed the boy's arm and began to admonish him for telling lies. "I would buy chiclets from an honest boy but never from a liar. You see how you have lost a sale by telling lies?"

"But I'm not lying, mister," the boy said, lifting innocent eyes to El Sol's face and beyond to heaven itself. "I ask you only to listen to me before you say I am lying. An aphrodisiac is a thing that makes you want to have sex, right?" The torero nodded. "And these chiclets, when you chew them, your mouth feels clean, right?" Again El Sol nodded. "And from your clean mouth flow wonderful juices that make your stomach calm, right?" Another nod. "And when your mouth is clean and your stomach is calm, you feel more like making love, right? That's why I call them aphrodisiac chiclets." El Sol gave the boy ten pesos and told him to deliver the entire box to Doris Miller's address.

It had been many years since the red-light or *foco rojo* district was declared illegal by a reform mayor. A stranger in town could no longer prowl the streets looking for a window with a red light. He was now forced to ask a cab-driver or a bartender; bellboys refused to direct tourists to the former red-light district, preferring to market their own girls. When El Sol arrived in town, it had taken him half an hour to find the district; the taxi driver who picked him up took a circuitous route to increase the fare. Now he knew the district as well as he had known the palm of his hand during his early adolescence. Girls nodded to him from doorways. A public-health nurse smiled at him as she hurried by. A madam called him by name. He felt very much at home.

"Right here," said Bisco, pointing to the Nights of Ecstasy Cantina, "is where my Maria learned to understand the stock market. The law of supply and demand here also rules. On payday her stock goes up, on Mother's Day it goes down. Saturday night there is heavy volume, but prices go down toward the end of the evening as the women get tired. Monday is a very bad day. It is here that a woman with a good head, like Maria, can learn to trade. Here, she tells me, she learned that it is better to be common than preferred. With such experience, how can she be anything but a success?"

"NIGHTS OF ECSTASY" the sign said over and over, blinking the message with Pavlovian expectations. Below it, strings of beads covered a doorway. The odors of astringent, cold tea, sweat, perfume, beer and distillates of the maguey cactus slipped out through the strings. Prices were posted on a board behind the bar:

MENU

STRAIGHT	$ 60.00 M.M.
HALF & HALF	$ 75.00 M.M.
SIXTY-NINE	$ 90.00 M.M.
ROUND-THE-WORLD	$100.00 M.M.
COSTUMES	On Request
ALL NIGHT	$350.00 M.M.
SHOW	$ 35.00 M.M.
SHOW & GIRL	$ 85.00 M.M.

NO PERSONS UNDER 14 ALLOWED
NO SADISTS
WE RESERVE THE RIGHT TO EXAMINE
    OUR CUSTOMERS

"You better ask for Maria," Bisco told El Sol as they went through the beads. "She don't like me bothering her here. The chief gets very mad."

El Sol nodded and went up to the bar, where he asked for Maria and was told that she was occupied. He gave the bartender fifty pesos. "I want to see her now," he said.

The bartender called to an old woman in a white nurse's uniform. "Tell Maria the time is up." The old woman slid out from behind her washbasin and headed into the honeycomb of small rooms behind the barroom. They heard her pounding on a door, shouting, "Time, time. Time is up. Hurry up in there." There was a noise from inside the room. In a moment, a fat man, dressed in his shorts and socks only, came running into the barroom. The girls made catty remarks about his breasts. "Thief!" he shouted at the bartender. "Cheat! Queer born in Monterey! I wasn't even in the bed yet."

"You should learn to move faster," the bartender answered, smiling under his mustache. "Now you see what a disadvantage it is to be so fat. I feel for you, friend, but we are all at the mercy of time."

The fat man pounded the bar. "I was in there less than a minute."

"Ahhh," said the bartender, raising a finger of enlightenment, "to you it was less than a minute. That is the tragedy of corporeal relativity: time speeds up in direct proportion to your avoirdupois. Therefore, a minute to you may be an hour to a thin man. You see the relationship? The intersection of mass and time is determined by the amount of mass that must move through the measure of time. Your minute is enormous, friend. Look how many of my minutes could fit into your minute." The bartender shed a tear. "Tragic, just tragic. You see how it shortens your life to be fat."

The fat man laid his head upon the bar and began to sob. His breasts flapped against his knees. The bartender reached over and patted his hairy shoulder. "Now, now, friend, all is not lost. We are not prisoners of our weight. Let me recommend a diet for you. Yes, a strict diet is the thing for you; it will turn your minutes into hours."

"Thank you," said the fat man, kissing the bartender's hand, "you've shown me the light."

Armero, who had been standing near the entrance with Bisco, nudged his companion. "What logic, eh? You know, man, before the syphilis I could not follow such a complex argument."

"We'll see," said Bisco. "I know fat men. My father was a fat man all his life. As a child, I used to walk in front of him, carrying his belly; that's how I got so strong. When I got bigger and there was no one to carry his belly, we used to plead with him to lose weight. Every time we asked him to go on a diet he said he would, but he didn't lose a pound. The last thirty-five years of his life he spent in the same chair. He ate all the time. Even when he slept he had hard candies in his mouth so he wouldn't be so hungry when he woke up. At the end, he ate horses. The day he died he had a gelding for lunch."

"He never had a disease?"

"Not a sick day in his whole life."

"Too bad," said Armero, "it could have saved him."

Maria Guadalupe emerged from the crib area still saying her beads. Her head was bowed in concentration. Her fingers fondled and shifted the beads with a practiced lovingness. When she finished the prayers, she greeted Bisco, then Armero. When she came to El Sol, she spit on him and screamed, "Lousy queer." Then she called to the other girls, "Look, Lala's punk, the one I told you about, the queer *novillero*."

A whore dressed in nun's habit threw an egg at him. "Hater of the Virgin!" she shouted. "Pervert! Anti-intellectual!"

"Wait a minute," El Sol said, covering his face with his arms to protect himself from the spittle and eggs and other objects aimed at him by the girls. "I went to Lala's house, but I'm not a queer; I'm an artist."

A buxom girl, clad only in a three-cornered diaper, squirted tabasco sauce at him out of a douche bulb. "Try to put us out of work, will you? Pig!"

"Whores of the Nights of Ecstasy, arise!" shouted a bespectacled girl with a mustache.

"Watch out now," Bisco called to El Sol, "she's the shop steward." But it was too late. The girls attacked, spitting, scratching, kicking, dousing him with cold tea, snapping garters in his face, clubbing him with washbasins and dildoes, and shouting: "Queer! You take away our overtime! Exploiter! Faggot! Depress the market, will you? Pig! How dare you put decent girls out of work!" They beat him until he was unconscious, crumpled on the floor in a swamp of tea and spittle, with a dash of tabasco sauce. "Get that queer out of here," said the shop steward. Armero and Bisco complied, dragging El Sol out by the arms, through the beaded curtain and into the street. A group of mariachis passed. "Look," said the *guitarrón* player, "must be a queer." They spit on him and kicked him a few times before they went on.

El Sol's friends dragged him into the privacy of an alley and waited for him to regain consciousness. "I'm sorry," said Bisco when the torero opened his eyes; "Maria Guadalupe is sometimes very difficult to get along with. She is a kind of fundamentalist, you know."

"Yes, I know—Christ, cunt and common stock." El Sol had difficulty speaking. He reached a finger into his mouth and fished out a round piece of flattened sponge. "Oh, that's better," he said. "I wondered what was causing the trouble. Ech, a whore's contraceptive," he said when his eyes focused on the sponge. "A disgusting thing, really disgusting."

"They don't understand you," Armero volunteered. "That's all it is, a misunderstanding."

Bisco agreed. "And I'll talk to Maria Guadalupe about it," he said. "She's a very sensible woman. That's why she doesn't understand you. A sensible woman like her has a big problem trying to understand an artist. You can see how that would be."

El Sol rubbed a garter wound on his cheek. "Why does it have to be that way?"

Armero patted his chest, thinking it was his back. "The whore also considers herself an artist. She's jealous. The only thing that disturbs me, friend, is that the whores think you are queer. I hate to think so, but the whore is the pure woman, the golden-hearted Eve. And whores know men; practice makes perceptive, you know."

"You think I'm queer?" said El Sol.

Bisco kicked at a can in the pile of garbage where El Sol lay. "I don't know how to tell you this, friend, but whenever a man decides to do something as dangerous and manly as bullfighting, there is always reason to be suspicious of his masculinity. I am not an expert in the field of psychology, but a friend of mine, who is now dancing with the Tijuana Ballet Company, had studied much. He tells me that everything known about the human mind is based on the case of Don Juan; that is, what is true is always the opposite of what is observed. As he says, who can deny logic? So you see, Solito, we hate to think you are a queer, but your masculinity, it gives you away."

4

Bisco and Armero went back to the Nights of Ecstasy to pick up Maria Guadalupe and take her to Delia's party. El Sol went back to his room to wash and change his clothes. He washed a long time before he felt clean again, then he lay on his bed and talked with Sam before he went on to the party.

He asked the cockroach to be frank with him and tell him whether he thought he might possibly be bisexual, if not entirely homosexual. Sam was unable to help. He explained that roaches did not suffer such problems. As creatures of instinct rather than learning, they had no choice but to be heterosexual. He referred El Sol to the case of the termite, whom he called his cousin. The termite, according to Sam, suffered from the problem of asexuality. He said it was a result of the corporate structure of the termite's life, with several queens at the helm, a few males to attend to their sexual needs, and the rest of the community devoted to unrewarding work.

El Sol asked if he was not taking a Marxist attitude. Sam denied it, claiming he left Marxism to the ants, cockroaches being existentialists by nature. He did, however, discuss the dangers of the corporate life at great length, basing his opinions both on his cousins and on humans who had been observed by the New York branch of his family. El Sol tried to lead him back to the subject, but Sam preferred to discuss corporate life or the general unhappiness of his cousins. When El Sol pressed him to find out why he would not discuss homosexuality, Sam finally admitted that he was afraid it would cast suspicion on their friendship. El Sol, laughing, said, "I wouldn't worry about it. A human and a cockroach can hardly have an overt sexual relationship of any kind, homosexual or heterosexual." Sam disagreed. After a long time he was able to explain to El Sol that he believed human beings were capable of the most outrageous forms of perversion.

5

Delia Monroe lived on an estate maintained by the Moloch Corporation as a tax loss. On rare occasions the company held sales meetings on the property. In 1946, when the corporation was converting from the manufacture of World War II weapons to nuclear and bacteriological warfare research and development, the main house had been built for several scientists, their patients and laboratory equipment. Later, a large infirmary for patients suffering radiation sickness and contagious diseases had been built at the back of the property, out of sight and hearing of the scientists, who did not wish to be distracted by the sounds of suffering. During the Eisenhower administration, the entire staff had been moved to a wooded area in Maryland, where they remained until 1963. At the end of that year, a permanent fifty-million-dollar facility was completed in Houston, and the scientists moved again.

There were, of course, no salesmen in the usual sense. The sales staff was composed of eleven U. S. Senators, 34 U. S. Representatives and 50 State Superintendents of Education. All of them were paid in cash, and their salaries simply reported as profit by Brazen Monroe ("Freckles" to the inner circle), who was granted a depletion allowance of ninety-six percent by the Eighty-third Congress. The' houses and grounds had been unoccupied from 1947 until early that year when Delia had decided to come to Mexico. Now it was filled with writers, party girls, painters, members of East Coast Society, civil-rights leaders, movie stars, and left-wing intellectuals. They came in a river of gaiety and obstreperousness, flowing through days and nights of gossip, dancing, drinking and serious conversation. Delia had dedicated the mansion to fun, and fun was had by all who entered there.

El Sol stood a long time in front of the wrought-iron gate before he pressed the bell. Over the gate it said in wrought iron scrollwork: "MOLOCH MEANS FUN."

He rang. Next to the gate a television screen lit up and Delia appeared on videotape. "Good evening," she said seductively, speaking in English. Spanish subtitles appeared on the screen just below her chin. "I'm Delia Monroe and I'm so glad you could come. In ten seconds the gate will swing open. Do come in. See you later, darling." She blew a kiss to the viewer, then the screen went dark. Six and a half seconds later the gate opened. El Sol stepped through and onto the carpeted walk that led up to the main house. Orchids bloomed along the walk, tape recordings of birdsong and the chirping of crickets played. Odors of rose and gardenia floated on the refrigerated air. Lights, like stars, twinkled overhead. Beside each grouping of lights was a small sign bearing the name of the constellation. El Sol was not sure whether he was inside or outside. He hoped for rain.

The door to the house was open. He could see people dancing and talking inside. "Come in," an electronic voice told him as he walked up the steps to the front porch. He told the voice, "Thank you." Once he was inside, he realized that he was very late and that it would be difficult for him to catch up with the party. In a far corner of the half-acre ballroom, not far from the redwood grove, he saw a young couple making love. Closer to him, a husband and wife were engaged in mortal combat. Several people lay unconscious on the floor, shoved out of the way by the dancers. In the center of the room, her blonde hair and black mantilla flying, Doris Miller demonstrated the gypsy art of flamenco. Her chin was over her shoulder, proudly. Her hands clapped and her heels beat the floor in random rhythms. Armero stood nearby in deaf devotion to her art.

He had been there for only a moment when Delia spotted him and came crashing through the dancers, shouting, "Hola, matador!"

"Hi," he said, bracing himself for a post-deb tackle. He grunted once when she leaped at him and again when she clasped him to her bosom. "This is your party, torero," she said. "This is the party before our party."

"Olé," he answered, still trying to recover the rhythm of his breathing.

"Let me introduce you to everyone," she said. He nodded. "Everyone," she cried, the sound amplified and fed through loudspeakers—there was a tiny microphone in her bosom—"everyone, everyone. Give me your attention, please. Our guest of honor has arrived. Here he is: El Sol de Michigan. Olé! Olé! Olé!" A hundred and fifty voices answered, "Olé! Olé! Olé!" The dancers waved their handkerchiefs, demanding that he be given an award. "Later," she answered the handkerchiefs, "I have a private award for him later." The dancers let out a precision snicker.

El Sol drew Delia close to him and whispered into

her ear, "Delia, please, everyone doesn't have to know. It'll cause trouble." As he finished the last word, Doris Miller hit him with her purse. The blow knocked his nose into Delia's ear. "Excuse me," he said, extricating himself, "I hope I haven't injured your cochlea."

"It's not really cochleary," she answered, giving him a pat on the cheek.

He turned to Doris, who was twirling her purse around her head as if it were the sling of David. "What's wrong with you? Why did you do that?"

"You're unfaithful; you deserve it."

"Listen, Doris, if I was faithful to you, I'd still be a virgin."

"And what's wrong with that? Just because you're a bullfighter, a big artist in the plaza, you think you can be promiscuous. You're all like that; every bullfighter is just a Don Juan under his Suit of Lights. And here I thought you were a family man."

"What are you talking about?"

"I'll show you," she said. "Armero, darling, will you make love to me?"

"Gladly," he said. "Where are you?"

She took the tip of his cane, which was groping dangerously near her face and led him away. With his free hand he continued to grope for her. She dropped the cane and gave him her left breast to hold, leading him out of the house.

Delia and El Sol watched them go. "Were you having an affair with her?" she asked.

"Only of the heart. Limited to the heart."

"But she always seems so willing. I always thought she was a regular little tart."

"Oh, no," he said, "she doesn't have the stomach for it."

Delia shook her head in sadness, then brightened and took El Sol by the hand to introduce him to her guests. In fifteen minutes of hand-shaking and good wishes for his coming *corrida*, he met Norbert Hert, the illegitimate son of the former ambassador to Bolivia; Christiana Pope, Countess of Tel Aviv; Nubbin Neuschatenwoorm, exiled Prince of Rumania; Erna Choyne, a fashion model; Tiara Barata, a Mexican film star; Contessa de Verguenza; and Hy Thighroyd, former head of the Department of Anthropology at Harvard, now a filmland columnist.

After the introductions, Delia led him to a corner. "As a famous matador, you should know that kind of people. You can't afford to be seen with people like that Indian Guero Talclantlan and that awful blind man. It isn't proper, really. The winners must never mix with the losers, darling; it's a law of nature."

"But my roots . . ."

She kissed him on the mouth. "Darling, you're not a tree."

"Well, I suppose, but I don't even know these people. If I wasn't fighting on Sunday, they wouldn't even talk to me. The other people were my friends before I ever had anything. I can't just drop them."

"If you want to be with the wonderful people, you'll have to drop them. Do you think you'll be invited to parties like this, if the wonderful people know you associate with blind men and Indians? El Sol, this is the acme of life. Do you realize that this party is being filmed by three different people and tape-recorded by two others? Future generations will look at this party and know this is the sixties. You can be part of them, El Sol, but to be with wonderful people you must be wonderful, too. Learn, darling, please. Drink, kiss hands, chat politely, catch up on the goings-on of the set. Never think it's gossip. It's history."

A tear fell from his right eye. "Why are you doing this for me?"

She gave his genitals a friendly squeeze. "Because I believe with all my heart that you have what it takes to be one of the wonderful people."

He wept openly. Bisco, who had been standing

nearby, picking the meat out of hors d'oeuvres, hurried over to him. "What's the matter, friend?" he said, laying a handful of mayonnaise on the torero's shoulder.

El Sol shook his head, still weeping.

"Listen to me, Solito, if anything's bothering you, just give the word. We have to stick together against all these rich bastards."

Delia nudged El Sol. "You cross-eyed fool," he said to Bisco. "These are my friends. Don't call them bastards, understand?"

Bisco backed away, tears in his eyes, too. "As you say, señor. I am at your service."

As soon as Bisco was out of earshot, Delia giggled in El Sol's ear. "Marvelous, just marvelous. You have real talent. That pig will never bother you again. Now you don't have to take any more favors from him."

"Yes," he said, taking her arm, "I can be with you all the time now."

"Of course, dear, all the time." She shook his hand off her arm. "But I have to circulate now. The guests. Mustn't monopolize the hostess, you know." And she was gone.

He looked for her through teary eyes, but she had slid into the crowd of dancers and vanished. He saw a girl in a leopard-skin dress doing the frug with a bald man in a wheelchair. Lala, wearing a sari and with a red mark on his forehead, passed the bald man in a leap. A dowager was carrying a young boy on her hump. He saw a man with a monocle crawl between the legs of another man who was wearing culottes and a turban, but he did not see Delia.

Nagadoches North, attired in the robes of an African prince, appeared at El Sol's elbow. "You look down, toreador," he said. "Please don't do that. My essay, you know. You have to go bravely. You have to be laughing right up to the moment the horn impales you. A god must be confident at all times."

El Sol turned to look at Nagadoches when he began to speak, but the small bone that pierced his nose and shone white against his cheeks so distracted the torero that he was unable to comprehend what he heard. "Mister North," he said, "there's a bone in your nose."

"There's a bone in everyone's nose."

"Yes, but the bone in your nose is an extra one; it's not natural."

"Because I am an Afro-American."

"What?"

Nagadoches rearranged the trailing end of his robe over his shoulder. "It is natural. Africans have worn such beautifying devices for thousands of years. I would say that it is natural to the dignified black man to wear a bone in his nose."

El Sol laughed. "Oh, I get it, you're making a joke. I forgot you were a black humorist."

North glowered blackly. "It's no joke. I forgot to tell you that I am a black nationalist as well as a black humorist. The Watusi are the tallest men in the world."

"What does that have to do with it?"

"I thought you should know that before you die."

"I'm not going to die," said El Sol.

"Just keep saying that, whitey; it's the perfect build-up to your punch line."

"And what's my punch line?"

"Death. Hah hah, hahahaha."

"And that was your punch line," said El Sol, driving his fist into North's belly.

Nagadoches bent over, holding his belly. "You Jews have always treated us this way," he said. "You made us miserable. You made us black."

"Now, wait just a minute, Mister North. We have nothing to do with your color."

"I know you're a segregationist; you don't have to tell me, whitey."

Lala jumped between them, landing lightly after performing an entrechat. "Boys, boys," he said, "this will never do. We must be friends. We must love each other."

"I thought we already discussed that," El Sol said.

"You may have another opportunity. Sunday has not arrived. I've not yet written my review. And I don't hold grudges, my dear. Well, not really."

He reached out to pat El Sol's cheek, but the torero stepped back out of reach. "I told you that I intend to have a good *corrida*. And that's enough."

"It's hardly a beginning, *divino*. Ask our literate friend here," he said, stroking the still bent back of the black humorist-nationalist.

"Watch out, Lala; I feel my mucus rising."

Lala grabbed North's arm, lifted him up and into a dancer's embrace. "Let us be off, little black one. Our friend has a nose for trouble." They kissed and whirled away into the crowd, robe and sari flowing, sandals flying.

"And you're a black pederast, too!" El Sol shouted after them.

He stayed in a corner by himself until the show was announced. Then, as the lights dimmed and a spotlight was turned on in the corner near the brook stocked with trout, he joined the crowd to see what was under the white cloth. A priest was brought on to bless the thing about to be unveiled. Mariachis sang. The three cameramen focused on the scene. Delia appeared in front of the veiled platform and spoke into the microphone in her bosom: "Wonderful people, we have a wonderful surprise for you. Our entertainment this evening is a demonstration of a gift that I will later make available to all of you. Please feel free to participate in the entertainment, if you wish. We would rather have a happening than a show. Remember, beauty is in the genitals of the participant. And now, here is Maria Guadalupe and Pato."

The left side of the cloth was lifted first, revealing Maria Guadalupe's face, then her hands and naked breast. She was saying her beads. Her eyes were closed and she was smiling slightly, spiritually. The cloth continued upward, revealing more and more of the naked woman, until her navel was exposed. Then, with a sudden motion, the entire covering was lifted and the figure of Maria Guadalupe being made love to by a blue duck was revealed. The platform tilted and turned slowly to further reveal that the head of the duck was immersed in Maria Guadalupe. The crowd applauded. An organ version of "Ave Maria" by Schubert poured out of loudspeakers above the platform and the audience began to sing. Halfway through the prayer, a former French film star began to quack. The music changed to the "Hallelujah Chorus." The people changed their song too, and soon all were singing, "QUACK quackquackquack QUACK quackquackquack."

El Sol did not sing. A woman who was standing next to him nudged him sharply. "What's the matter? Don't you know the words?"

"It's not that," he said. "I don't sing that song; I'm not a Christian."

The woman edged away from him and turned back to watching the performance, singing more loudly than before. On the platform Maria Guadalupe was straining at her beads and the duck had started to flap its ineffectual blue wings. The music stopped, followed by an end to the quacking. The room was silent but for the flapping of the duck and the mumbling of Maria Guadalupe. The amplifiers hummed. The onlookers shuffled expectantly. Then there came from Maria Guadalupe a long groan, amplified by the sound system into a roar that set everybody in the building to quivering. The onlookers embraced each other and lowered themselves to the floor as the veil descended over Maria Guadalupe and the now prostrate duck. El Sol searched for Delia. He could hear her breathing through the loudspeakers. Obviously, he thought, she was also searching for him.

He found her against the front wall in a dark place shaded from the lights of the room by bent coco palms. Gringo Salazar, the pickpocket and sometime *novillero*, was with her, his hands running over her body with the delicacy of a policeman searching for weapons. While he performed the caress, she looked over her shoulder into the main part of the room, her eyes searching the prone couples for El Sol.

"But I thought . . ." said El Sol, stepping through the palms.

Salazar, who had earned his nickname by scrupulously limiting his activities to American pockets, continued to caress Delia with his left hand while he pushed El Sol away with the other hand, incidentally stealing his wallet. "Go away, Feldman, find your own woman."

"We had a date. Isn't that right, Delia?"

"I also had a date with Gringo."

"Which date did you make first?"

"The one with Gringo."

"You see," said Salazar, pushing El Sol again.

"It's very clear," El Sol said, nodding in agreement, "she made a date with you before she met me. Then, after we met, she preferred me to you, so she made the date with me."

Delia stepped away from the two toreros and lit a cigarette, preparing to watch the inevitable combat. "You may as well fight now," she told them. "I can't wait all night for you."

Gringo and El Sol glared at each other. They moved around the small clear area until El Sol's back was to the wall. Gringo, seeing an opportunity, lowered his head and charged like a bull. El Sol waited until the pickpocket-torero was almost upon him, then he stepped to the side. Gringo crashed into the wall and fell unconscious to the fern-covered ground. A trickle of blood ran from his scalp.

El Sol turned Gringo over and took his wallet out of the pickpocket's pocket. He looked at Delia. "Shall we go now?"

"Oh no," she said, "not yet. You've had a marvelous *corrida*. You deserve a trophy."

"Please don't make jokes about it. He might be badly hurt. I really didn't want to hurt him."

Delia reached into her hair and took out a long knife. "As judge," she said, "I award you one ear. Olé! El Sol!"

"And why don't I deserve the tail?" He was laughing.

"Your capework was not all that I had hoped for," she said, bending over Gringo and pulling his ear away from his head to make a clean cut.

6

Delia led El Sol to a small room on the third floor of the house. It was furnished with monastic asceticism. The bed was narrow and made of thick oak planks. There were bars over the small high window. Next to the bed was a simple wooden chair and beside it a small chest. The light bulb in the middle of the ceiling was unadorned. "It's the way I prefer to make love," she explained to El Sol, who showed surprise at the decor. "Sex must never be anything but pure. Colors, slinky fabrics, oversize beds, music and those other gimmicks are only dilutions, at best. And sometimes they're used to escape the truth of a man and woman alone with only their bodies to depend on. Without accoutrements passion is on display. Sex is naked."

"I may as well tell you now," she went on, stepping out of her dress, "that most men fail in this situation. Don't feel too badly if you do. Your manhood won't be permanently damaged if you fail here. After a year or two, you'll try with other women. Of course, you'll know what you really are if you fail here, but then why should we deceive ourselves? We must know truly how well we perform."

"Do you give grades?" El Sol asked.

"No. There is only passing and failing."

"Do you think I'll pass?"

"Take off your clothes, toreador, and we'll see."

"Well, if you think I'm not going to make it, I'd rather not try. You know what I mean, I'd just as well be deluded. Two or three years is a long time."

Delia removed her slip and unhooked her garters. "I can never tell. Men have failed who I would have bet my life on. It's not the easiest of situations. But when it works, and every once in a while it does work, it's marvelous."

"Did it work with Gringo?"

"Every time."

"But you weren't satisfied with him?"

She gave him a toothy grin. "I'm never satisfied. Now, get undressed. Aren't you anxious to find out about yourself?"

"Well, up until now I've been pretty confident, but now I don't really know. Maybe we should call the whole thing off?"

She switched off the light. "We must eliminate the possibility of you getting excited by looking at me. Voyeurism is failure." She removed the last of her clothing and lay on the bed. "Hurry up, El Sol, I'm curious."

"Yes," he said, and took off his clothes.

He waited until his eyes became adjusted to the near darkness before he walked across the room to her bed. In the dim, indirect moonlight that shone through the small window he could barely make out her features. "Delia," he said, getting onto the bed, "you're very beautiful."

"I know."

He kissed her and fondled her, preparing to make

love. He was ready to be tested, he told her, and he was looking forward to it. Suddenly, he leaped away from her. "Delia," he shouted, "you have two vaginas."

She gave a low chuckle. "I prefer it that way. It took me a while to get accustomed to it, but now I'm very happy that I had it done."

"You weren't born that way?"

"Of course not. My father suggested the operation after my second affair—it was with a Negro. He told me a girl of my class should have two vaginas if she wanted to explore some of the more exotic people. One is for my kind of people, the right one, and the other is for dark-skinned people and that sort of thing, the left one."

"And you always do it that way?"

"Certain lines," she said, "must not be crossed."

El Sol lay down beside her again and began kissing her. "And which one is for me?"

"I've been thinking about that," she said. "You're not dark-skinned and you're not poor, which would put you in the right. But then, you're an artist and you *are* Jewish, aren't you?"

"Yes."

"That would put you on the left."

He stroked her thigh. "What difference does it make?"

"Don't be ridiculous, darling. There are rules, you know, rules of conduct. It's important. Daddy said it is, and Freckles is a very smart man."

"Well, what do you want me to do?"

She shook her head. "I don't know. I'm really terribly concerned."

"Look," he said, "I have an idea. Instead of going left or right, I'll do a little on one side and then a little on the other."

"Anarchist bastard!" she screamed, and crossed her legs.

8. YOUR SON, THE SUN

The typewriter Sol brought with him to Mexico was stolen the same week he lost his camera, radio, phonograph, and electric razor. During his second week in Mexico, his gold fountain pen was stolen. After that, he wrote with fifteen-cent ballpoint pens or fat pencils. He had settled down on his bed with a ballpoint pen in his hand and a thick magazine on his lap for a desk, preparing to write a letter to his mother, when Sam stepped out from under the dresser.

"Hello, Sam," the torero said. "Say, I'm pretty busy right now; I wonder if you could come back later. I really want to get this letter off to my mother." He turned to the paper on his lap and began to compose the salutation, but in the corner of his eye he saw Sam, who had not returned to his place under the dresser. "All right," he said, "let's talk for a while, but not too long. I haven't written to my mother in weeks; she'll worry."

They spoke about mothers first. Sam explained that cockroaches had a better life than humans because they had no relationship with their mothers. Some cockroaches, he admitted, were troubled by egg fixations, due mostly to difficult emergencies or lack of sufficient protein while in the egg, but the other neurotic problems that humans suffered because of their mothers were unknown to cockroaches.

"I love my mother," El Sol told him.

Sam trembled with what the torero could only assume was laughter. He, of course, did not know of love, was not troubled by it. As an egg-born animal, he was able to be entirely rational. He commented on the slow maturation of humans and the waste of perfectly good females through morbid devotion to child rearing. Mother love, in his opinion, was the cause of war and art, the most obvious manifestations of human irrationality. When El Sol pressed him, he admitted that war, in the case of hunger as the cause, was not always entirely irrational. Art, he maintained, was totally neurotic, useless; it could not be eaten, nor could it protect one from the elements or his enemies; it was not logical. From his point of view, love, art and war were a result of the conditioning of the young human to mother love prior to his emergence into a hostile world. The egg, on the other hand, being neutral did not cause emotional dichotomies that give rise to such unnatural acts.

"Love is an unnatural act?" El Sol asked.

Rasp.

"We would do better to hate?"

Double rasp.

"Oh, so we should just leave each other alone?"

Rasp.

"So why don't you quit bothering me and let me write this letter?"

Sam, hampered by his limited vocabulary, was forced to retreat. With drooping feelers, he turned away and walked back to the dresser, stopping on the way to pick up a crumb of decayed orange peel. He remained at the edge of the shadow, chewing on his tidbit and occasionally emitting a double rasp, which El Sol ignored.

It took several hours for El Sol to compose the letter to his mother. When he had finished writing it, he settled back on the bed and read it over, pencil in hand, poised to correct mistakes in spelling or to fill in the accidentally omitted words.

Friday eve.

DEAR MOMMA,

I am fine. How are you? How is grandma Victoria Regina and the rest of the family? What is the weather like up there? I hope it has been good. I hope it has not been too hot or you finally got air-conditioning in the house. Were there many mosquitoes?

I am very excited these days as I am about to make my debut in a very big bullring this coming Sunday which is a break bullfighters hope for all their lives but few get because they are not good enough or do not have the right connections in the bullfighting circles in Mexico. I joined the union.

It would be very nice if you could come to my debut as it is the most important day in my life since my Bar Mitzvah or the day I graduated grade school because it marks the opening of new doors for me in a new stage of my life and career. If you came to the bullring on Sunday I would put my fancy (for show not for bullfighting) cape up by your seat in the first row shady side which I would get for you and you would be very proud I hope. As it is right now I don't happen to have a girl I am dating regularly so you would be the one who got the seat and the cape (the fancy one) which is considered a big honor for a woman. I'm not kidding.

You shouldn't worry about me and bullfighting because its not so dangerous as they say in all the books and movies especially now that the Mexican doctors are so good with antibiotics and the bullfighters are smart and don't eat anything but tea and a little brandy on the day of the bullfight just in case. Also the horns of the bulls are not so big as you would think especially compared with a Texas longhorn cow or something like that.

They are more like plain ordinary steers that you get in the meat market.

Anyway I am not afraid because I practice a lot and have a really good teacher who has told me practically everything you need to know about being a good bullfighter. The thing that really worries me about the bullfight and the debut is that I might not do such a good job and that I might not get any more contracts in the big bullrings and have to go back to fighting again in those little baseball parks that they turn into bullrings or in those little towns where they don't have good doctors and it really is dangerous if you make a mistake or have an accident. As I am an artist now I also worry about doing the art in a first class way because a second class artist is not an artist as I have written to you before in these letters but only a foolish man who might get hurt and embarrassed for no good reason at all in the bullring if you know what I mean by that.

I have met a lot of nice people here who are very friendly to me including a few girls like Doris and Delia who had a party last night in her big house that I went to and had a very good time. My Mexican men friends are really pretty nice guys too like Hijo de Quien and Bisco and Gringo Salazar and the famous bullfighter of yesteryear Armero II who has told me a lot about the history of the art of bullfighting and given me some pointers about how I can be better in the bullring for my debut on Sunday. My other friend Sam of whom I told you about in previous letters from here is also around a lot and a very good friend though he is smart and interested in some philosophical ideas which I do not understand completely and sometimes disagree with though I often try to listen to his advice because he has a lot of advantages in the way he thinks and I don't just take him lightly.

The weather here is very hot in the daytime and not too cool at night when it gets down around 85 sometimes after it is over a hundred in the day, which is a lot hotter than I ever got used to in Michigan but not as bad as when I was traveling in Texas and Arizona where it was over a hundred all the time and my car used to be as hot as fire when I got into it after a sales call.

I hope you are glad I am becoming an artist and trying to make something of myself in the bullfighting career because I know how sad you felt when I didn't go to college and learn a trade like my cousins and most of the other boys in the neighborhood, but you have to understand that artists are different and take different ways to getting their success as many famous artists who did not finish high school have said in the past and keep on saying even now.

Although I didn't go to college I still read a lot especially about bullfighting and the books by Hemingway who I started to like if you remember the time when I started to like to read when I was very young because he is a very smart man and knows a lot about bullfighting which he writes about in the way that I am writing this letter to you with a kind of tough way of talking about things but not with any dirty words like some writers use now or any phony stuff. My typewriter got lost.

There is not much to do here in the daytime but the nights are quiet and I have noticed also that a lot of these people are very poor which makes me sad but not too much because I think that they have a lot of spirit besides being poor and really don't suffer too much except when they are hungry and at times like that or in the wintertime when it gets doggoned cold and they really could use electric blankets even the old kind without the individual side controls but they don't miss electric blankets because they have no electricity which is a blessing as you can see because of their situation. There are a lot of shoeshine boys in Mexico.

I am surprised that you did not get the lace mantilla or the perfume or the silver platter or the shoes made of alligator skin or the purse or the blouse or the serape or the watch or the pottery that I sent to you because everytime I went to a store and bought one of those things the people promised me to send it to you by airmail as soon as I left the store which is very nice of them and makes me think there must be something wrong with the mails or else there is an international problem. There is a gorgeous silver coffee set in one of the stores here that I admire a lot and know would be perfect for your canasta club when they come over. I'll send it special delivery so there won't be any problems.

As regards elimination. It is not a problem for most people in Mexico because of the food or the climate or something but I can tell you for sure that the people here really eliminate regularly and some do it too much which is something I never thought of before I got here so don't worry about me being regular. I eat a balanced diet.

I have to go now because I'm going to be interviewed for a magazine which is very interesting to me because I have never been written up before. So take care of yourself and be well and Grandma too.

Love,
Your son
EL SOL

9. DEATH IS NOT A BARGAIN: THE LATE E. HEMINGWAY REJECTED

Irving Mitch, the famous writer, was sitting at a dimly lit back table in El Macho, the men's bar of the old Hotel Cojon, cutting pages out of an old book with a razor blade and pasting them onto numbered sheets of blank paper. El Sol recognized him by their prearranged sign: a white silk tie and a white on white shirt. The torero carried a copy of Mitch's last book *The Arab Mistress,* a fictionalized life of Abraham which included a detailed account of the sex act that caused Sarah to conceive after her ninetieth year. On the dust jacket there was a portrait of Abraham looking like a hirsute Rudolph Valentino. El Sol had not read the entire book, only pages 759 to 831, the description of the sex with Sarah.

"Mr. Mitch," he said upon arriving at the author's table, "I'm El Sol, the torero from Michigan. I read your book; would you autograph it for me?"

The author gripped his cigar tightly in his dentures and swept the book and papers into an alligator-skin attaché case. "Sit down, sonny, sit down. Have a little drink, kills the amoeba. Sure, I'll autograph the book. No charge to a famous toreador, hah ha."

El Sol pulled out a chair and sat down, ordering a beer from the waiter, who had hurried over at a snap of the author's fingers. "Here's the book," he said, setting it on the table with care. The author took a broad-tipped gold pen from his inside coat pocket and wrote: "To my dear friend and bullfighter. All the best from Irv."

"Thank you," said El Sol, blowing on the ink to dry it, "but what are you doing in Mexico? I read in Mike Connelly that you were in Hollywood writing the movie script of *The Arab Mistress*."

"Finished it, finished it. Got out a hundred pages last week and the studio loved it. I watch for their stock to go up ten points the minute the word gets out it's a masterpiece. Now I got this little piece to knock off for Cosmo before I really get down to brass tacks and do some work. Actually, I'm materializing down here, but keep that to yourself, huh, kid; I promised it to Winchell. The readership's important. Can't have that kind of thing lost in a three head on an AP story. Nobody reads the goddamn papers anyway these days. Christ, if it wasn't for television . . ."

"Oh, I won't tell anybody. I wrote to my mother, but I didn't tell her your name. She's a fan of yours; it wouldn't be good for her heart. Is it hard, what you're doing down here?"

The author belched and shivered. "You'll pardon me," he said, recovering his breath, "this Mexican chicken liver. No, it's not hard to materialize, just a question of sticking to it. I'm doing the life of Montezuma; *Aztec Harem* is the working title. Yesterday, just yesterday I counted the steps on a pyramid, and right at the top—I was so out of breath I thought I'd bust— I came across a little slit in the steps where they must have let the blood run down from the sacrifices. That's the kind of detail that makes a book great. You can almost see this Aztec prince standing on the steps while the virgin he loves is about to be sacrificed, and he knows all the time her blood is going to run right down the steps past where he's standing. Then, I pick him up two chapters later, he's still standing on the steps but the ceremony is just about to where they're going to sink the crooked dagger into her heart, and he draws his golden sword. Your heart skips a beat when I tell you about it, huh?"

"It certainly does."

"Aha!" said the author, raising a finger, "but did you know he was bisexual? Did you know he loves the priest as much as he loves the girl? Save the girl or kill the priest? You see, a book is more than just action, there must be conflict, emotion. Of course, for the movie version the priest will have to be his brother. Tab Hunter. Tab Hunter is the prince. You got the picture? A golden-haired Aztec. I'll have every snatch in Westchester itching."

"I read that menopause causes itching in that area."

The author pulled a piece of wet tobacco off the end of his tongue and dropped it into El Sol's beer. "Look, sonny, I'm down here to do you a favor; don't get smart with me. You know how many people'll read this article about you? You'll be worldwide, see? Now, watch your mouth or I'll Pearl Harbor you, but good. You understand? Okay, now tell me how you got started in this bullfighting and talk slow, I'm making notes."

"I'm sorry if I made you angry," El Sol said, trying to fish the piece of tobacco out of his beer with his forefinger. "I didn't mean to."

"Let bygones be bygones. Now, give, what's the story with you and this bullfighting?"

"Well, I guess I got interested in it because I'm from up in Michigan. When I was in high school I read a story about that—where I'm from—by E. Hemingway, the writer. It was the first story I really liked since *Evangeline* by H. W. Longfellow, the poet. Anyway, I got to reading books by E. Hemingway and *The Sun Also Rises* really got to me, that bullfighter, Romero, you know. So I read the *Death in the Afternoon* and I never forgot it, it made such a deep impression. I really wanted to go out and *torear* and *banderillar*. Sometimes I'd lay up half the night just thinking about honor and courage and things like that. I'd dream about being able to *aguantar* and *miedo* and all that stuff. The more I read by E. Hemingway, the more I wanted to be a man, and the more I knew a man wasn't a man until he got out somewhere and tested his courage; you know, saw if he was really a man or just a sissy or something. I wasn't afraid of the wolves around town and killers didn't bother me much. I wanted to know what really is happening, what's true, you know. What's art and that kind of stuff: So I figured if E. Hemingway was only a high-school graduate and I was almost one that I could be an artist just like him. That got me to thinking about death and being a man and I decided I could really face up to death if Sidney Franklin—he's still my idol because E. Hemingway said he was okay—could. So I gave up the life of a sissy out there on the road selling stuff to the Negroes for their hair and decided to test myself in the true way, like E. Hemingway would have said, you know, against death. And that's how come I came down here and saw a bullfight and knew right off that the *corrida* was the place for me to find out."

The author lit another cigar. "Yeah, so what do you think about death?"

"You mean just plain death or violent death?"

"Gimme a few words on both kinds, huh? I'll edit later."

"Well," said the torero, smiling as he pulled the piece of tobacco out of his beer, "death can be okay. Say you're old, fifty or something." The author shuddered visibly. "I'm sorry, make that seventy," El Sol said.

"Yeah, that's a little better. You don't want people to think you're a kid."

"Uh huh," said El Sol, holding his story until the author had finished brushing a hunk of cigar ash off his tie. "Well, say you're very old as I was saying. If you say that, you have to say that death is okay. It's coming, you know, and you might as well just take it because you have cataracts and no prostate and heart trouble. Life is no picnic when you're old and sick. Once you lose your health, what the hell, that's what E. Hemingway must have thought, don't you think?"

"I don't know. He was a hunter. I don't catch on to him. The only thing I ever hunted was gash. Hah ha! You get it?"

"Sort of," said El Sol, managing a chuckle. He sipped at his beer, which tasted of Havana bad breath. "Well, back to death," he said, "Now there's old death and young death. Old death is just what has to happen, but young death is diffcrent. Young death is in two parts. No, better make that three. First, there's accidental death. We can't do anything about that. Then there's dying well and dying badly. Say I'm out there in the bullring and I'm scared and running from the bull, can't keep my feet in one place, and I get gored. That's dying badly. But say I'm making a beautiful series of *naturales* and I finish off with a *forzado* and the wind comes up suddenly and I get it. That's dying well. You see what I mean? If you have your pride when you die, it's not so bad. You're a man, you know. You have to shit in the boots of the Virgin or your life is no good because your death is bad. And you have to do it truly, not just say it."

The author finished his notes, puffed out a cumulus cloud from Cuba, and settled back in his chair. "You know what Ernest said about death before he died? He said death was a whore."

El Sol was stunned. "He said that?"

"Before he died."

"It doesn't make any sense, Mr. Mitch. Death can't be a whore. You make bargains with whores. You give her money and she screws you. You can't do that with death. If E. Hemingway said that, he was wrong. Death is no whore, Mr. Mitch. I've been out there pretty close to it and I can tell you that death is true, the purest thing there is. You can't fool around with death, believe me. And if E. Hemingway said that, which I'm not so sure he did, then he wasn't true to himself."

"Look, sonny, the man had cancer."

The torero stared into his beer. A tear ran down his cheek. "I don't care," he said, sobbing. "He wasn't a good and true man if he said that."

The author waited until El Sol was able to control the sobbing, offering a scented purple handkerchief to wipe away the torero's tears. He ordered a fresh glass of beer for him and did not season it with wet tobacco. Then, perceiving the end of the crisis in El Sol, he leaned across the table and whispered, "Listen, kid, the thing that's going to make this article a smash is sex. You see, people wonder a lot about you bullfighters. Now, be honest with me, kid, and don't be embarrassed; when it comes to *shtupping,* have you got any new wrinkles? You know what I mean: a new position, some words you say, some little thing you do that maybe nobody else does. C'mon, you owe it to the public. Details, the public, the fans, they deserve a little intimate stuff."

"That's too personal."

"Once you step out there in front of the crowd, sonny, nothing's too personal. They want to know. Maybe you had a bad circumcision. Maybe you like a little Greek style, huh? Give, baby, for your audience. If you don't tell, they'll make it up; I'll make it up. I'll give you a one-inch *putz* and undescended testicle. Don't hold back or you'll be sorry, very sorry. You can be figured out, you know. Maybe you're a fag, like Huckleberry Finn. What do you think about that? C'mon. How long can you last? You got any special foreplay? What do you think about lubricants?"

The torero shook his head.

"All right, all right," said the author, leaning even closer to El Sol, "at least do me a favor. Where's a good whorehouse in this town?"

10. WHEN THE SUN GOES DOWN, THE MONEY ROLLS IN

After the interview, El Sol went to La Monumental to eat a bowl of *menudo* and admire the buttocks of Consequencias the waitress. He had difficulty eating the soup in her presence. Once, while lifting a spoonful of *menudo* to his mouth, she passed by his table. Abandoning one appetite for the other, he turned to watch her and spilled hot soup in his ear. In his embarrassment, he pretended he had been annoyed by a fly, complaining aloud that it was unsanitary for a restaurant to be situated over an open sewer. The manager, who was standing behind the cash register, padding the charge accounts, pretended not to hear him.

El Sol had finished his soup and was devoting himself to observing Consequencias when Macho Davila, the lady bullfighter, entered and came to his table. She smelled of cow dung as always. He wondered if it was on her boots or her jeans or perhaps embedded somewhere in her leather jacket, like a sachet. El Sol had often participated in speculations about the odor of Macho Davila. He and the other bullfighters had passed many hours that way. The most popular theory had been advanced by Armero, who claimed she used it as a cosmetic, the way a famous Mexican actress was said to use the semen of young boys. El Sol found all the theories unsatisfactory. He hoped one day to ask Macho about her odor, but so far he had not had the courage to do it.

Macho pulled out the chair opposite El Sol, turned

it around so that the back of the chair was facing him, then straddled the seat and sat down heavily. El Sol breathed through his mouth. "I hear you're going to test your balls this coming Sunday," she said.

"My balls are okay," the torero answered; "it's my luck I'm worrying about."

"You have balls, you have luck."

He watched her mouth, attracted by her mostly gold teeth. "I hear you had a *corrida* a few weeks ago in the baseball park in Tortillera. There was nothing in the papers afterward, or else I missed it. How did you do?"

"A goring," she said, rising and beginning to unbuckle her belt, "but it's not bad now. Look." She unbuttoned her pants and let them fall to her knees, revealing jockey shorts underneath. El Sol looked at the crotch and was relieved to see that it was empty and puckered. She started to lower the shorts.

"Not here," he said, "please."

She dropped the shorts far enough to reveal a fresh scar on the left side of her belly just below her navel. "What does it matter between us?" she said. "Now, look at that scar. From a fucking calf. Two hundred kilos and it leaves a hole like that."

"Put your pants on," he said.

"Wait a minute, man." She motioned to Consequencias to come to the table. "Look at this scar," she said to the waitress. "Some *corrida*, eh?" Consequencias blushed and backed away. Macho smiled and reached for the waitress' buttocks to give them a slap, but Consequencias slid away, graceful as a fat tap dancer. "You make me blush," she said. Macho laughed loudly. "Don't act like a waitress all your life." Consequencias left to return to the kitchen and Macho pulled her pants up and began buttoning them. "I'd like to get into her pants," she said.

"So would I," said El Sol.

Macho glared at him. "You're not man enough."

El Sol might have argued with her, but he remembered too well the night in El Tapatio when Bisco had pushed her into a fight and then, after twenty minutes of mutual pummeling, had been forced to settle for a draw. "Well, I have to go," he said. "I'm glad your wound is healing and you feel okay."

"Thanks," she said, giving him a cursory salute. "Hey, on Sunday, man, don't forget your balls."

"I won't."

"I mean it," she said. "For killing, you kill with your balls."

Back in his room, he undressed and crawled into bed. It was not late, but he was tired. When Sam emerged and asked if he wanted to talk, he was not happy with the idea. "I'm too tired," he said. "This has been a difficult day, a difficult week, and Sunday's not so far away anymore. Maybe it would be better if we waited until tomorrow."

Double rasp.

"You think it's better if I talk, huh? Maybe I'll unwind a little?"

Rasp.

He told Sam about the interview and the visit with Macho, complaining all the time, demanding to know why he couldn't be alone and in peace, a bullfighter and nothing more. The life of celebrity which he had only just tasted made him unhappy. He complained about being inspected, poked into, tested for things that had no bearing on how well he could fight a bull. "I feel naked," he said. "I am afraid of what will happen if I have a good *corrida*. They'll take off my skin, too."

It is the fate of bullfighters, Sam told him, along with adulation, mutilation, misunderstanding, and an early death. He urged him to give up bullfighting for a more reflective or constructive activity: criticism, carpentry, philosophy, astronomy or television repair. No one but a few toreros would ever know what he really accomplished as a bullfighter, but everyone enjoyed television, stars, cabinets, God and destruction. He pointed to Lyndon Johnson as an example.

"I am loyal to my President," said El Sol, which so upset Sam, who held vegetarianism to be the most sacred belief of civilized beings, he withdrew from the conversation and returned to his place under the dresser.

"Good night, Sam," said the torero, chuckling under his breath, because he was not really loyal to his President.

In the morning, he was awakened by Suitcase Morales, who shouted his name and pounded on the door. "It's time for the *sorteo?*" he said in answer to the pounding.

"No, you dumb bastard," Morales said. "The *corrida* is tomorrow. My General is here now; he wants to see you."

El Sol threw off the ragged quilt and rough cotton sheet. "I'm coming," he said, going to the door, rubbing his eyes and feeling the need to urinate. As soon as he unlocked the door, Morales pushed it open and stepped aside to allow the general to enter. "Good morning, My General," the torero said, bowing slightly.

The general, dressed in the clothing he wore when participating in horse shows with the Mexican equestrian team, strode into the room, snapping his riding crop against his boots. "Good morning, good afternoon!" he said. "Why do you sleep so much? After the *corrida* you will sleep. You will sleep like the dead." He laughed, Morales laughed louder.

"I don't expect to die," said the torero, hunting for his slippers, which he found under the dresser. After he put them on, he said, "Excuse me, please, I have to urinate."

"The fear," said Morales, slipping the torero's ballpoint pen into his pocket.

"No, the night."

"You are afraid of the dark?" said the general.

"I don't piss in my bed," El Sol said and went into the bathroom.

"Ah," said the general, "but when you see the bulls I bought with your five hundred dollars, you will piss in your pants."

"I've seen big bulls before," El Sol answered, his voice coming hollowly out of the tiled room.

"One has horns long enough to impale three men at one time on one horn and it's blind in the right eye," said Morales, putting the torero's electric razor into his pocket, then finding the bulge too big and setting it back on the dresser.

"I have no fear."

El Sol turned on the shower for a moment to wash away the urine, having learned to use the shower for a urinal since the toilet had been stolen. He walked back into the room, looked at his electric razor, smiled at Morales, then asked the general why he had come to his room. "To bring you this form," the general said. "It is for the insurance, two hundred and fifty thousand pesos. Did you ever think your life was worth so much?"

"And who is the beneficiary?"

"Sanchez-Villa, Sociedad Anónima."

"That's you incorporated," said El Sol.

The general smiled. "It shows how much I value your life." He put the paper on the dresser. "Now, sign it please, right here."

"And if I don't?"

The general frowned. "What kind of man are you? Here I have given you the chance for a glorious suicide and you would deny me a small profit from it. Only an American could be so ungrateful, only an American Jew."

"Now that you put it that way," said the torero, "I'll sign." He looked around for his ballpoint pen. "Morales," he said when he realized what had happened to the pen, "give me the pen."

"I swear I am innocent," said Morales. "My General is my witness."

The general reached into the breast pocket of his khaki silk shirt and produced a pen. "Here, don't bother Morales; use this."

El Sol signed the form. "I hate to do this, because it's going to cost you a lot of money. I'm not going to die tomorrow."

"You will, you will. Don't try to upset me, Feldman. Tomorrow, when El Sol goes down, the money will roll in. Believe me, these are your last hours." He laughed. "And now that death is so near, have you any last words?"

"Morales owes me a ballpoint pen. Pay it and do not neglect it."

"That," said the general, "shall be done. But see if you have anything else to say." To this question El Sol made no reply.

11. NEVER EAT WHEN YOU ARE
HUNGRY—A TOLTEC PROVERB

In the afternoon El Sol went to the Plaza Freg and stood in the dangerous territory in the center of the sand. Hijo de Quien watched him from the shadow of the gate of *cuadrillas* but he did not speak to him. Later in the afternoon, the caretaker told Bisco, "He had the look of death on him. Don't bet against the general." Bisco replied that he imagined the torero was thinking of the olés or planning his *faena*. The caretaker was adamant. "I was there. I saw him. The boy knows. That is the worst part, man; his death will be no surprise."

The cross-eyed picador shrugged. "Maybe you're right, man. After all, you saw him."

They went to the corrals to look at the bulls, which had been unloaded early that morning. Three of the animals were small. Their horns were closed. The spare bull was no more than a calf. But the fifth animal was enormous, with a giant *morrillo* and wide, open horns. "They should shave the horns," said Hijo de Quien.

"How do you know that will be El Sol's animal? Maybe Morro will draw that one?"

The caretaker laughed and scratched his genitals. "I know My General."

Bisco picked up a clod of dirt and crushed it in his fist. "I know, the big fucker will make sure. But if the boy brings that bull to me, I'll put in the *vara* right down to its guts. It will be half dead before the *banderillas*."

"And what if the judges change the act before you have a chance?"

"Well," said Bisco, "what if he charges like a train?"

"And what if he doesn't see so good from one eye?"

The picador shook his head and kicked dirt, his eyes trembled, moving dangerously near his nose. "We should get a priest."

"For a Jew?"

"Who knows?" said Bisco. "Perhaps in his last moments we can save him forever?"

The caretaker patted Bisco's shoulder. "Even a butcher," he said, "can be a moral man."

2

For several days Armero II had been planning to visit El Sol on Saturday afternoon to explain to him that it was better to be booed and whistled than to die. He had prepared a speech about the foolishness of *naturales* with difficult animals and the inability of the crowd to see exactly how close he was taking the bull. During his years in bullfighting he had learned to cheat the danger, and he planned to divulge his secrets to his young friend on that afternoon. Most of all, he wanted to tell the young torero how to kill from the side and make it appear as if he had gone in right over the horns. "There are secrets," he had mumbled to himself during those days, "ways to survive."

He was on his way to the Hotel Xochimilco when two lady tourists offered to buy the drinks if he would tell them about his career. That night, drunk and weary, Armero rose from between the flesh of the ladies and demanded his clothes. "I must see El Sol," he said. "I have to save him. He is too brave, too brave."

"Find them yourself," said the ladies, giggling.

"I can't, I need help. I'm drunk and blind. I don't know which end is up."

"That's why we love you," said one of the ladies.

"That's why we won't let you go," said the other.

"You will be sorry. In ten days you will know of my revenge," said Armero as the ladies presented themselves once again. The ladies giggled.

3

The device was made with two discarded picador's lances, eight shopping bags, and hundreds of feet of fuzzy brown twine. The ends of the lances were padded and shaped to cling to the shoulders of the bearers. Guero and Panzona deposited one child in each shopping bag, then lifted the ends to their shoulders, adjusted the pads slightly, admonished Jesusita to walk alongside to slap the children who fouled their bags or attempted to escape, and set out for La Monumental, where they were to have dinner with El Sol. During the six-block journey, Guero attempted to sell one of the children to an arthritic matron, who declined the offer, insisting she could and would have one of her own the moment the hot Mexican sun cured her sufficiently to enable her to uncross her legs. Guero suggested she visit a doctor, whom he knew to be a specialist in amputations, for the immediate removal of one of the offending limbs. "Never," said the matron, hurrying away in quick, efficient scissors steps.

Guero shrugged, which nearly threw two of the children out of their bags. "What is one to do with a mystic? There is still much work to be done by International Masonry."

Outside the restaurant Jesusita left off slapping the children to tell Guero that she did not intend to pay for the meal out of the money she was saving for her debut in Hollywood. "I wish you would," he said. "I would do anything to keep you from going to that corrupt place. But there is no need to worry; El Sol, the matador from Michigan, has invited us. He is a very rich man due to the timely death of his father. On this penultimate day of his, he chooses to share his anxiety with us. You will therefore show him the respect he is due by not soliciting during the meal." He spoke slowly, choosing his words carefully, blonde hair shining in the evening sun, black eyes glittering, his slim body drawn up to his full height of more than five feet.

"All right, old man," Jesusita answered, "but remember, please, that every trick I miss means another half hour I must wait before I join Marilyn Monroe and Maria Montez."

"She has a one-track mind," said Panzona.

Guero scratched his head. "Perhaps a lobotomy . . ."

Jesusita held the door open for them and Guero and Panzona marched into La Monumental, Panzona's feet splashing in the rivulet of urine left by the children. El Sol was sitting at the back of the room at the head of three tables he had pushed together to accommodate his guests. Jesusita ran ahead and threw her arms around his neck. "Ohhh, *matador*," she said, preparing her mouth for a kiss. "How kind of you to come," the torero said, averting his mouth.

"You don't kiss whores?"

"I don't kiss little girls on the mouth."

"I am not a little girl anymore. I have a pubic hair."

"When you have bosoms."

"*Mamarracho!*" she said. "You call me a little girl and you are not even weaned."

"Behave yourself," Guero told his daughter as he lowered his end of the litter to the floor.

She kneed him in the groin. "Youth must be free," she said. Guero fell onto a chair, massaging the in-

jured area. "You see, Papa," she said, "we are not like
your generation." She spit on him once, waved to El
Sol, and left.

"Gall bladder," Guero gasped. "Enlarged. I must get
her to a surgeon."

The other children were hung on the backs of chairs
and dinner proceeded. They ordered fried stomachs for
the children and *nalga de Tijuana* for the adults. The
fried stomachs were wrapped in cactus leaves and
covered with chocolate and vinegar sauce. Consequencias brought them first. On the next trip she
brought the rump steak in green chile sauce to the
adults. "Jesus Christ, I'm hungry," said El Sol as the
plate was set in front of him. "I haven't eaten all day."

Guero put his knife and fork down. "Then you
shouldn't eat."

"What?"

"It is an old Toltec proverb," said the maestro.
"Never eat when you are hungry. There is no blood in
your stomach when you're hungry. You could be poi-
soned by the food."

El Sol made a sour face. "Guero, if I can't eat when
I'm hungry, I'll starve to death. Can you tell me how
to get around that?"

"I am not a physician," said Guero.

The torero ate lightly, confessing that he was not so
hungry after all. Guero was relieved at his removal
from danger and changed the subject. Panzona's
health was worrying him again. She appeared to be
pregnant, which he thought unnatural since her uterus
was in a jar in Guadalajara. He turned to her with a
crafty smile. "Perhaps my Panzona has not been faithful to me."

"I have always been faithful," she said. "Look how
our children resemble you." She called them each by
name, "Uno, Dos, Tres, Cuatro, Cinco, Seis, Siete,
Ocho."

Guero thrust out his lower lip with pride. "I don't

know. Cinco is very tall for her age. You are lucky, Panzona, that she is the twin of Seis, the little one." He laughed.

One of the children became ill. Panzona gave her a *jalapeño* to soothe her. "The fried stomachs," said Guero, "are not too easy to digest. Similarity repels. An eye for a tooth is better."

After dinner, they lit up cigars and settled back in their chairs to discuss the coming *corrida*. Panzona, a dutiful wife, left the men to talk while she amused the children by blowing cigar smoke in their faces. Guero explained a system he had invented for drawing the best bulls; then he discussed the torero's bowels. El Sol admitted to slight constipation. Guero clapped his hands and bounced several times on his chair. "Constipated! Marvelous. You see, you are an artist. You are holding your art within you until the proper moment. It is a sign."

"Do you mean . . ."

"It is nothing," said Guero with a wave of his hands. "The greatest artists, in their moment of creation, have known it. Have you ever noticed the poor clothing worn by artists? As you can see, matador, it is foolish for the artist to wear fine clothing if he is a true artist."

"This happens to all artists?"

Guero nodded gravely. "It is a law of physics."

12. THE FATEFUL SWEATBAND

El Sol slept very little the night before his *corrida*. He passed the early part of the night going over his checkbook. In the past year he had earned five hundred pesos, forty American dollars, as a bullfighter. His expenses were five hundred dollars for the coming *corrida*, seven thousand one hundred and seventy-two dollars for doctors and hospitals, a hundred and twelve dollars for initiation and dues to the union of bullfighters, and fifty payments of ten dollars a week to Guero, who rented the use of the plaza for practice. He did not include as losses the money spent for a Suit of Lights, dress cape, *capotes, muletas, ayudados* and swords: eleven hundred and fifty-three dollars. He listed that under capital assets rather than investment spending.

Around midnight Sam appeared and spoke with him for several hours. He suggested that the torero feign illness and avoid the *corrida*. No afternoon, no matter how beautiful, he told El Sol, was worth a man's life. The torero argued that he did not expect to be killed, but Sam would not listen. In his logical, artless mind the death of the torero was imminent. Art is a form of suicide, he claimed, the giving of one's life to an illusion, by which he meant the audience existed and appreciated only in the imagination of the artist.

El Sol became angry. "Without art or sex, the way you live, what is there? You can only observe and criticize."

Rasp.

"That's no way to live."

Double rasp.

"All right, it's a way to stay alive, but not to live. Besides, if there was no art and no sex, you would have nothing to observe. The world would be dead."

Double rasp.

"The world would be logical."

Emphatic rasp.

"I couldn't bear that."

Sam retired in silent disgust to his place under the dresser. El Sol lay in his bed waiting for the dawn. He was hungry, but he knew he could not eat; they might have to operate. He turned on the light and began a letter to his mother:

> DEAR MOMMA,
>
> In a few hours I will be making my debut in the Plaza Freg and I am scared to death of it because everybody keeps saying that I am going to die which I don't want to do in case I had a future as a bullfighter the thing I have always wanted. What can you do when you want so much to be something and do a good job and be a real artist and everything and it might cost you

He tore up the letter and went back to bed. It was almost dawn when he fell asleep. He had nightmares about anti-Semites and bad reviews. Later, when he was exhausted by the fearful dreams, his unconscious soothed him with visions of the right vagina of Delia Monroe. At ten o'clock in the morning, while El Sol still slept, Guero kissed each of his children, gave Panzona a loving rectal examination, and left for the *sorteo*.

They were all there before Guero arrived. Hijo de Quien had opened the gate for Despreciado Alvarez and Pimienta Gomez, the managers of Mata Morro.

Bisco and Armero had come next, followed by Suitcase and the general. They did not speak to Guero when he arrived, but immediately began the business of the *sorteo*. Hijo de Quien took off his hat, each of the managers spit in it to ward off evil spirits, and the general threw an American cigarette into the hat to bring riches to the toreros. Guero offered to shit in the hat for the sake of art. Hijo de Quien declined.

They went to the adobe wall of the corrals and looked over the animals. The small, brown ones were called Palomo, Suave, and Sincero. The extra bull was called Chapo. The giant animal with the open horns was black with a green rump and was known as Fregador.

"We have paired the animals," said the general. "Fregador and Palomo, Suave and Sincero." Suitcase glared at the group. "Any objections?"

"Fregador is too big," said Guero. Despreciado agreed.

"Fregador is an opportunity," said the general. He turned to Suitcase. "Put it in the hat."

"I'll take the first paper," said Despreciado.

The general shook his head. "The first must go to Guero, a courtesy to his Yanqui matador. Where are your manners, Despreciado?"

Guero watched Suitcase mark two papers, examined them to be sure one said Fregador and the other said Suave, and waited while Suitcase turned his back and put the papers into the hat. "God of the Shriners, God of the 33rd Degrees, God of the Eastern Stars," he prayed, walking toward the hat held out to him by Suitcase, "let me keep my friend and benefactor alive." He closed his eyes, turned his face heavenward for a moment, then dipped his hand into the hat. The inside was damp with spit. Pieces of tobacco stuck to the silk lining. He felt one piece of paper, tucked it into his palm and searched for the other. There was only the cigarette and the spit and the folded square of paper in his palm. "Bastards!" he shouted, "there is only one paper."

The general smiled. "Calm yourself, you little son of a whore. Feel around. Maybe you'll have some luck. Otherwise, my indigenous friend, take what you have."

Guero shrugged, felt around the bottom of the hat again, and came up with nothing more. Then a smile came over his face, and he reached his fingers up into the hatband and began feeling around the circle of the hat. Halfway around, he encountered the second square of paper. He grabbed it, and suddenly laughing, jumping into the air, he shouted, "I have the second one! I have the right one!"

Bisco, Armero and Hijo de Quien joined in the laughter, converging on Guero and slapping him on the back. "Read it," said Armero, "read the paper."

Guero opened the folded square of paper deliberately, pausing after each fold, making a ceremony of it. At the last fold, he spat for luck, then pulled it open so sharply the paper snapped. "FREGADOR."

The general started to leave the entrance to the corrals. He waved his pigskin gloves at Guero. "Until four in the afternoon, rabbit."

"You are a dishonest man, My General," said Guero.

The general rubbed his mustache, smiling. "No. You are the dishonest one."

"I am innocent," Guero protested.

"The fate of an innocent man is in the hat, not in the sweatband. I know you, Talclantlan. I knew what you would do, because I have studied the quirks of the Masonic mind. The blood of El Sol is on the fezzes of your brothers."

13. IT IS USELESS TO PISS ON
THE TOES OF A FRIEND

At noon, El Sol was awakened by an argument between Bisco and Maria Guadalupe. "You remember," Bisco was shouting, "the man who gets it free off you is a man I'm going to break in half. I will not tolerate perfidy of your love."

"Goat, nothing was free. He gave me a tip on the market; I gave him a little extra without charging."

"See," Bisco screamed, "see. Perfidy. Fucking perfidy. And you're defending the bastard, too. I'll find him, Maria, and when I do, I'm going to let him have it right in the mother."

"You know how much money I made from that tip?"

"It's not the same," he shouted. "It's not business!"

El Sol formed a megaphone with his hands and shouted, "Shut up! Kill each other, but do it quietly. Come in here, I'll give you a knife."

"Oh, your friend, the queer, is awake," he heard Maria Guadalupe tell Bisco. There was the sharp sound of a slap repeated several times. After that it was quiet, until he heard the bed creaking and he knew Maria Guadalupe had regained her fidelity, even her virginity in the crossed eyes of the man who loved her. He rolled over and tried to sleep again, counting the squeaks of the bedsprings to lull himself out of consciousness, but the squeaking stopped before he was asleep. He looked at his watch, saw that it was after noon, and decided to get up. "Not even four hours," he said aloud. He yawned and yawned again.

It was not stuffy in the room, he knew, because there was no glass in the window next to the dresser. He yawned again.

"Sam," he called, "Sam." The cockroach did not appear; it was too light in the room. El Sol walked about on the tile floor, accidentally stepping into a rotten papaya he had left for Sam and cursing loudly. He scraped it off his foot with a piece of paper and went into the bathroom to take a shower. There was no hot water. There had never been any hot water in the Hotel Xochimilco, though the manager always promised a modern Japanese hot-water heater, installed before the first day of winter. He also promised windows, a chair in every room, and although he made no promise to repair the roof, he did swear to put a pan under every leak at no extra charge. That was important because El Sol had requested pans for the leaks in his room during the last rainy season and had been billed fourteen pesos extra for every week he used the pans —one peso for each pan.

He turned on the shower and stepped back to allow first the green and then the brown water to empty out of the pipes before he began to wash. It always amazed him that such cold water could be so filled with microscopic life; it did not correlate with anything he had learned in high-school biology about the habits of the unicellular, but then things were different in Mexico: Sam was no ordinary hexapod, for example, and the Mexican amoeba was certainly a singularly hostile creature. The shock of the water made him wince. He shivered all during the shower and for some minutes afterward.

An hour later, the visitors began to pound at his door, the tourists who came to watch the ceremony of dressing the matador. Before the afternoon was over, he or Guero politely turned away more than fifty people, including the East Texas Flagpole Sitting Champion; the Grand National Paraplegic Baton Twirler (second place); two members of the Tampa, Florida, Mounted Sheriffs' Posse; the principal of Venus Hill High School, who had been with Armero on Saturday night; Novale Verga, who appeared in her Miss Bisbee, Arizona, of 1942 crown and carried soggy papiermâché scepter; Coriolanus Schwartz, a Ph.D. candidate; Al Capone's favorite grandniece; the assistant editor of the *West Coast Steamfitter's Journal;* and Miss F. D. R. Larue, retired queen of burlesque, inventor of the Depression Grind, and holder of the only lifetime W. P. A. grant.

Guero arrived shortly after one o'clock. He carried his Suit of Lights, his *montera* and his *capote* in a sling made of thick cotton cloth. He also carried a coffee can full of chicken soup. "It is for you," he told El Sol, presenting him with the hot can. "Panzona and I have been studying your religion. We are thinking of becoming Jews, you know; Panzona has already bought a book of interest rates."

El Sol thanked him for the soup. After spooning the rust off the surface, he ate half of it. "There is more to being Jewish than chicken soup and interest rates," he told the maestro. "For example, do you know anything about chopped liver?"

"It is not necessary," Guero said. "I do not intend to become Orthodox."

The next to arrive was Bisco. He was dressed for the *corrida*, except for the armor for his left foot, which he would not put on until he was in the plaza. He and Guero unpacked the torero's uniform and his swords. While Guero took the cloth outer covering off the Suit of Lights, Bisco sharpened the swords. He continued to work with the sharpening stone while the maestro dressed. He put on four pairs of stockings to hide his skinny calves. After each article of clothing was on and secured, Guero went to the bathroom to urinate. On the third trip, El Sol went, too. In his nervousness, the torero aimed badly and urinated on the

toes of the maestro. Guero jumped back the moment
he felt the warmth through the four pairs of stockings.
"Be careful, man," he said. "You can only cure athlete's foot with your own urine. It is useless to piss on
the toes of a friend."

"I'm sorry," said El Sol. "I wasn't trying to cure your
athlete's foot; I'm just nervous."

Guero clapped him on the back. "It's nothing, matador. I am only telling you because it is a fact of medicine and a fact of life. There are limits to friendship,
and we must live them. In the plaza, when the bull
charges, I can't help you."

El Sol nodded, "What you say is true. I never
thought of it, but in the moment of truth there is no
one to piss on your toes but you yourself."

"And it is also true when you make love to a woman," Bisco called from outside.

They laughed and smoked and urinated away another hour. Armero arrived and Hijo de Quien stuck
his head in to wish them luck. They could hear the
band outside the plaza playing *pasos dobles:* "La Gachupina," "Malagueña Miedosa," "Huevos" and "El
Gitano Fregado."

El Sol yawned. "Fear," said Guero. "Death," said
Bisco.

"What happened?" Armero said. "I didn't see what
happened." He became excited and began to tap
around with his cane, shuffling about in a circle.

El Sol took his arm to calm him and led him over to
the bed, where the blind man sat down. "I yawned
again," El Sol told him, "that's all."

Armero's head fell forward and he covered his eyes
with his hand. He groaned and rocked mournfully.
"Sex," he said, and moaned again. "Sex is the undoing
of all toreros. The greatest of *faenas* has been lost in
the bed the night before. These *peones* and picadores
do not understand that. They have not been alone in
the plaza with the crowd and history watching. No

one can know but the matador. And I, matador, tell you, friend: sex is the enemy of *tauromaquia*. And that is why you yawn, El Sol, because you have left the energy of your art in some woman."

"I haven't been with a woman for nearly two weeks," said the torero.

The blind man nodded. The muscles of his face slid into a sneer. "You lie, El Sol. The signs are unmistakable. You have screwed away your career. In a few hours you will see, man: you screwed yourself."

"Don't listen to him," Guero said. "His brain is sick with syphilis. It should be removed." He grabbed Armero's arm. "C'mon, vulture, get out of here. El Sol will have a great afternoon. He is an artist, a constipated man, whose art will flow from him like a river when he fights."

Armero struggled, striking wildly with his cane at the half-costumed *peon*. "Not art, but blood will flow from him this afternoon. The general is right. He screwed himself. The general is right."

"Enough," said Bisco, who had been sitting on the windowsill, watching and listening, waiting for his opening into the conversation. In two steps he crossed the room and stood before Armero. The cane hit against him, but he did not even flinch. Armero lowered the cane and sat quietly. "You are a traitor to your friend," Bisco told him. "You feel jealousy, that's your trouble. That's why old matadores spend so much time with people like Lala, because they get to think like them. Lala always wanted to be a man; you were once a man, and you would like to be a man again. That's the truth, isn't it?"

"No."

Bisco grabbed Armero by the throat and began to strangle him. "That's the truth, isn't it? Say that's the truth."

Armero struggled at first. As his face turned from cinnamon to grape, he gasped, "Yes, yes."

"You see," said Bisco, relaxing his hold on the blind man's throat, "the truth always wins out in the end."

"Of course," said El Sol, stifling a yawn.

The torero was about to begin dressing for the *corrida* when there was an authoritative knock at the door. Guero opened the door a crack, and a manicured hand passed in a white calling card. Guero read the card. "It's Sr. Riendo of Inhumaciones Riendos."

"Should we let him in?" El Sol asked.

"He is a very rich man," Guero whispered. "Perhaps he would like to become your patron."

They opened the door and Sr. Riendo stepped into the room, bowing slightly and smiling greatly. He wore a morning coat and spats. "Good afternoon, gentlemen," he said, "I am here to make the arrangements."

"For what?" said El Sol.

"For your funeral, of course."

"I am not dying."

"Such modesty," Sr. Riendo commented, laughing. Then a wave of seriousness, beginning in his gray temples, came over him. "But there is no need to be modest with me. To be a torero is to die; if not this time, then the next. You must have a funeral befitting your contribution. And fortunately, the Señorita Monroe has offered to provide you with the very best. What a lucky man you are! You must have pleased the señorita very much."

"You see," said Armero. He started to say more, but Bisco reached out for his throat, and at the touch of the thick fingers Armero became quiet.

"There won't be a funeral," said El Sol.

Sr. Riendo shook his head. "It is just as I told her: only the dead are grateful. Believe me, gentlemen, as one who has experienced both sides, I can tell you quite honestly that the living are nothing but trouble, while the dead are so tractable, so sure of themselves, they are a pleasure to deal with."

"I know what you mean," said Armero, "I would be willing to accept such an offer."

Sr. Riendo explained that it was possible for the funeral to be transferred to the blind man. He reached into his left spat for a contract, producing a long paper with congenital carbons and quickly marking it with x's and o's. El Sol signed wherever he saw an x, and Armero was guided to sign the places marked with an o. After the signing, Sr. Riendo tucked the paper back into his spat and patted Armero on the back, telling him, "You have done a wise thing, my friend. Now, you are a man with a future."

When Sr. Riendo had gone, Armero said to El Sol, "You are too young now, but when you grow older you will believe the old saying: The destiny of wine is piss or vinegar."

"And which are you?" Bisco asked.

"I am not a critic, in spite of what you say, picador. I don't know and I don't think about it. I leave it up to the taste buds of history."

It was getting close to three o'clock when El Sol finally got to the arduous dressing. He put on the knee-length underwear and three pairs of stockings, then the brocaded pants. He waited while Guero and Bisco stretched a towel between them. Straddling the towel, he pulled the waistband of the pants up while they lifted the towel between his legs, forcing the pants up tight in his crotch. "You wear your balls on the right?" asked Bisco.

"No," said the torero, "it's more comfortable on the left."

Bisco dropped his end of the towel and clapped his hand to his forehead. "God! No wonder you are gored so much. Don't you know the tradition?"

"Sure. But what difference does it make?"

The picador was so astonished his eyes became momentarily uncrossed. "You think traditions are without reasons? Belmonte, Joselito, Manolete, Arruza, Dominguin, Ordoñez all wore their balls on the right and you wear yours on the left! Hijo! The general knows, the general knows. Maybe there is still time to change my bet."

"It's that important?"

Bisco paced the floor, stuttering. "Explain it to him," he asked Armero. "You have the syphilis, you're the thinker, explain it to him."

Armero sighed as if he could concentrate his logic by deflating his chest. "El Sol," he began, "I want only to help you. It is very late now so you must listen very carefully and answer honestly. First, I ask you: Have men ever flown like birds?"

"No."

"And when men have tried to fly like birds, what has happened to them?"

"They failed."

"This failure, what did it do to them?"

"It hurt them; they got broken bones and things like that."

The blind man smiled. "And have matadores ever worn their balls on the left?"

"No."

"Then to wear balls on the left is like trying to fly. It will result only in failure and injury, right?"

El Sol shrugged. "I never thought of it that way."

"Never thought of it that way!" Guero shouted. "Crazy, we're trying to save your life."

El Sol pulled his pants down, shifted his testicles to the right side, pulled the pants up again and stepped over the towel. He groaned as they forced the silk up into his crotch, and he had difficulty when he tried to walk. They told him not to worry, that he would feel no pain when he faced the bull. He went on with the dressing. Guero folded several sheets of newspaper and tucked them around his knees, holding them there while he snapped the bottoms of the trousers together and tied them. He held the white, ruffled shirt for the

torero and helped him button it. Together, they but-
toned the tight, high-waisted pants, and Guero held
the sash while El Sol spun into it. "Matador," Bisco
said, holding the vest for him to slip into. El Sol made
his own tie, then brushed his hair back for Guero to
attach the pigtail. "I wish it wasn't called a pigtail," he
said.

Bisco helped him on with the heavy jacket while
Guero set up a small altar on the dresser and lit a candle. He knelt before the altar and began to pray. "I
thought you weren't Catholic," said the torero.

"I am not," said Guero. "It is only a tradition." He
crossed himself and got to his feet. Then they took
turns going in to urinate. El Sol yawned. The band
had moved into the plaza; they could no longer hear
it.

Bisco settled the picador's hat on his head and put
the leather strap under his chin. "You do not pray?" he
asked El Sol.

"When I have the *montera* on I'll pray."

"Where is your altar?"

The torero held the *montera* before him, calculating
how to put it on without mussing his hair. "We have
no altars. We pray to a God we can't see."

"Whew!" said Bisco.

"Don't make such noises," Armero said. "It is the best
god, the intellectual one; only the Jews and the syphi-
litics have such a god."

El Sol put on the *montera* and mumbled a prayer,
his head bowed. When he looked up again, they asked
him, "Are you afraid?"

"I shit in the boots of the Virgin," he said.

"These Jews," Bisco whispered to Armero, "even
when it comes to blasphemy they cheat."

14. A BULL NOT SEEN AT NUREMBERG

They walked down the long, unroofed corridor of the hotel and out into the street. El Sol strained to smile. He measured his step and held his head up, feeling the *montera* rakishly low over his eyes. "E. Hemingway," he mumbled, "you were right. If you can get death like this, it is a bargain." Guero followed him, walking slightly to his right, carrying the dress cape, his *montera* reaching the torero's shoulder. Then came Bisco with the heavy basket of big capes and *muletas* dangling easily from one hand, and finally, Armero tapping and carrying the swords under his arm. They marched, three slim men and the great, cross-eyed picador. Guero's stockings were falling around his skinny legs, Armero's fly was open and the seat of Bisco's pants was open at the seam, but El Sol, leading the parade, was unaware of them as he stepped out of the hotel and into the sun.

Women sent kisses at him, shoeshine boys flipped peso coins to him, beggars offered him their collections. A man with no legs stood up to cheer him. From the sidewalk a figure dressed in mourning with a dried-apricot face arose and offered to make love to him. Blind men said he looked splendid. He only smiled and put his hand before his face, gesturing toward them with it in the style of kings and matadores. Flowers fell on him and were strewn in his path, a rose thorn pierced his slipper and lodged in his foot. He tugged at the ache in his crotch. A girl fainted.

He turned to Guero. "I feel like Humphrey Bogar. Who do you feel like?"

"Guero Talclantlan."

"You have no dreams?"

"I dream only of beautiful women and gre surgeons."

El Sol shook his head and walked on. They crosse the street and stepped up onto the sidewalk in front the plaza. Soon they were in the shade of the o building. Hijo de Quien ran out to meet them. H wished them luck, then took the basket of capes fro Bisco and ran back into the plaza. They could he the crowd and smell the bulls. Bisco clamped a hu hand onto the torero's shoulder. "Don't worry, ma when I finish with that big one he'll have such a ho in the *morrillo* he won't be able to toss salad."

"Don't. Please."

"What's happening with you, man? You want die?"

"I am an artist. I feel it in my bowels."

"You're full of shit," said the picador.

"Yes."

Bisco ran ahead to finish dressing, mumbling, "C zy gringo." As he passed Guero he said, "A Mason a a gringo is too crazy. Maria Guadalupe was right should have gone short on him."

In the gate of *cuadrillas* they met Mato Morro a his manager coming out of the small chapel. Cone the *banderillero*, was still in the chapel, prostrate fore the Virgin of the Macarena. Mato smoked and cussed his coming trip to Spain with his manager. T *monosabios* were leading out the picadores' hor and the bigger horses that would drag out the de bulls. "How's it going?" El Sol asked Mato.

The *novillero* smiled, "If I had drawn that Fre ador, man, I would be going to Spain right now. Y can't kill an armored car with a sword."

"I'll get good reviews."

Everyone laughed. "Lala has already written your review," said Despreciado. "He showed it to Mato last night. It says you have the courage of a castrated lizard and the grace of a three-legged pig. According to him, your style smells like a rotten papaya."

"He has no honor," said El Sol.

Despreciado laughed again. "And you have no future."

Guero draped the dress cape around El Sol's left shoulder. The band was silent. The crowd began to applaud. "It is time," said Guero. "How are your bowels?"

"I have to urinate," said El Sol.

"It is too late."

"I'll piss in my pants."

"Courage, matador," said Guero, slipping back into the ranks of the *peones*.

The band played "La Virgen de la Macarena." The crowd became quiet. The picadores mounted their horses with much clanking and grunting. The inside of El Sol's right leg grew warm, then cold. There was a dark streak on the blue silk. The last trumpet note ended, the crowd applauded, and the man in black velvet with the feather in his hat spurred his horse. El Sol turned to Mato Morro, who stood next to him, smoking the last of a cigarette. "Good luck," he said.

Mato flipped the cigarette away and blew out smoke. "You pig, you pissed in your pants." The horseman backed his prancing animal into the shade, then out again. The band played. El Sol stepped out into the sun, smiling, swinging his right arm, walking with all the arrogance that could be mustered by a man who had just wet his pants.

The plaza was not filled. There had been more people at his Bar Mitzvah. He looked at the crowd, many of whom seemed already to be rooting for the bull, searching for someone who would display his dress cape. In the first row on the shady side he could see

Delia Monroe, and farther over in the less desirable seats was Doris Miller. Delia held a bouquet of roses before her, dipping her nose into them whenever the wind blew from the sunny side. She wore a silk dress and drop earrings that rested on the seat beside her. Gringo Salazar sat next to her, munching fried grasshoppers.

El Sol gave his dress cape to Doris Miller. "For the day when your stomach doesn't bother you anymore," he said. She took the cape from him and settled it over her shoulders. She tried to tell him something, but he was already too far away to hear, moving toward his place opposite the gate of bulls.

Guero gave him one of the big capes. "Don't step out until I get back, Solito. Let me see what kind of animal this is." El Sol nodded. They watched together as the gate of the bulls was opened. They waited, looking into the blackness of the long passageway. Fregador charged out, leaping as he saw the sun and felt the brown flag of the Tío Pedo herd planted in his back. The bull appeared to have grown overnight. It was as tall as a horse, with forelegs like an elephant and horns that barely cleared the passageway. The crowd gasped, the vacuum setting up little dust devils on the sand. Guero turned to El Sol. "How are your bowels?"

"Weak."

The *peon* nodded. "That's a bull!"

The general leaned down from his seat above the place where El Sol and Guero were standing. "Adiós," he said, stroking his mustache and grinning whitely.

The bull made a circle around the ring. El Sol felt the ground shake as he passed. On the second turn around the ring a *monosabio* leaned over a *burladero* and slapped his hand on the wood. Fregador stopped, skidding on the sand. The *monosabio* slapped the wood again and Fregador charged, hooking at the wood with his left horn. The horn went through the wood, splintered it, and came out again. "You are lucky," Guero whispered. "I think he's a brave one. It's the cowardly bulls that are unpredictable."

Mato Morro moved up next to El Sol. "Well, pisser, he's going to kill you. No one can kill such a bull, especially not a gringo." He laughed.

"Why laugh?" said El Sol. "If he kills me, you'll have to finish him off."

Mato opened the left side of his jacket to reveal a small pistol. "I am prepared."

"You can't do that," El Sol said, shuddering as the bull passed him again. "They'll kill you if they find out."

"How do you think I got the name Mato? I've been doing it for two years and no one knows."

"Now I know."

Mato grinned. "Yes, but I think it's a secret you'll carry with you to the grave."

Guero nudged El Sol and told him to pay attention, then he slipped out from behind the *burladero* and ran after the bull, shouting, "Eh, toro!" Fregador slowed down, came to an easy stop and faced Guero. Half the length of the plaza separated them. Guero called to him again. Fregador charged and Guero ran. It was a race to the fence. Guero dropped the cape in order to run faster. He reached the fence as the bull reached him, hitting him with the side of its horn and sending him flying over the fence and headfirst into the wall. Guero lay where he fell. There was a cut on his head and his left arm was twisted into a strange position, broken in two places above the elbow. Two *monosabios* brought a stretcher. El Sol ran to his side. The little *peon* opened his eyes and spoke in a weak voice to his pupil, "Don't worry about me. You must piss on your own toes anyway."

"I have," said the torero.

Guero's eyelids fluttered. "Yes, I forgot." His eyes closed for a moment while the *monosabios* lifted him onto the stretcher, then opened again. "Listen, Solito, this Fregador, he is almost blind in the left eye. Take him only on the right side. The right side, you hear me?"

"Yes, maestro. I'll be all right. You worry about yourself."

The *banderillero* smiled bravely. "I have always looked forward to major surgery."

The crowd was whistling and hooting, demanding that the *corrida* continue. "I have to go now," El Sol told Guero, "the crowd."

"Listen to me, my son, there is an old saying in this business of fighting bulls: The crowd can put the horns on you, but the bull can put the horns in you. Remember that." He managed another pained smile and gave El Sol the secret Masonic handshake for luck before he was carried off.

Conejo, the praying *peon*, gave El Sol his cape and asked if he could place the bull for him. "Away. And in the middle third," said the torero. "For *veronicas*." Conejo ran around the alley outside the ring and waved his cape at Fregador from the safety of a *burladero*. The bull moved toward him slowly. When he reached the proper area Conejo disappeared, and the animal was left in the requested place.

The matador stepped out from behind the *burladero*. He walked with a pronounced limp due to the painful placement of his testicles and the piece of rose thorn lodged in the bottom of his foot. The crowd settled into quiet. He approached the bull, took a position, and opened his cape. His head was tilted, his back was elegantly curved in the first stage of the *veronica*. He called to Fregador to charge. The bull came, fast and straight. El Sol made the *veronica* slowly. His feet were still. The crowd chanced a few olés. El Sol turned to take the bull again. He leaned out farther with the cape to extend the action of the pass. Again Fregador charged straight and fast, turning away from the torero just as he reached the cape. El Sol took the bull again and again, ending with a *media veronica* that startled Fregador into a tight, painful turn that left him standing bewildered in the center of the ring. The matador walked away, limping less, trailing the cape in the dust behind him. He had never heard such cheers.

The trumpet sounded the entrance of the picadores. El Sol leaned against the fence, talking to Hijo de Quien while the blindfolded horses were spurred to their positions. "Don't try for the tail," the caretaker said. "You can be careful now and still cut an ear." El Sol was about to answer when Fregador charged the first horse. The picador's pole broke off in the bull's back as it hit the horse and drove it through the fence and into the wall. The horns worked in the belly of the horse with mechanistic viciousness, shredding its bowels. When the *peones* were finally able to lure Fregador away, the horse was dead. On the other side of the ring Bisco laughed and waited his turn. He sank the *vara* deep into Fregador's tossing muscle before the bull hit his horse and lifted it into the air. The horse went down on its side, but Bisco held onto the end of the pole, swaying eight feet in the air in front of the bull's horns. The bull lowered his head, then charged upward at Bisco, the action causing the long pole to act as a catapult. Bisco flew across the ring and landed in the twenty-seventh row on the sunny side between the legs of a matron in menopause from Vermont, who was sitting with a nineteen-year-old boy from Vera Cruz, her guide to the night and day delights of Mexico. The woman clamped her legs around Bisco and began rocking to and fro, whining to her guide, "Why can't you do things like that?"

By the time Bisco was able to free himself, the judges had called for the picadores to leave the ring and the *banderillas* had been placed. The judges again called for the act to be changed. El Sol asked permission to kill the bull and received it. He dedicated the bull to the crowd.

El Sol intended to keep his work clean and classical. He approached Fregador slowly, intending to make a series of elegant, leisurely *derechazos*. The bull refused to charge. El Sol moved closer, stamping his foot, calling to Fregador, and shaking the *muleta* in the bull's face. When he was only a foot from the horns, Fregador looked up at him and whispered, "Do you know zat I am a Cherman?"

"I thought you were Mexican."

Fregador pawed the ground to cover his conversation. "Also I am aware zat you are Jewish, Herr Feldman."

"God help me," said El Sol.

"No, no, please, Herr Feldman. You are not zinking correctly. It iss to your benefit. I am of ze new Chermany. I vos never a Nazi, und I am very guilty over ze terrible crimes against ze Jews. To atone for zis sinful doings of my countrymen, I vish to allow you to have ze greatest bullfight ever. Do votever passes you vant, und do not vorry from ze horns. You are ze beneficiary from my guilt."

"Thanks," said El Sol, "I have always believed in the innocence of the German people."

He stepped back and held out the *muleta* again. Fregador charged straight and slow, following the *muleta*, docile, inches from El Sol's body. It went that way for several minutes, pass after pass perfectly executed by a fearless matador with a totally dominated bull. El Sol, in the glory of olés, changed the *muleta* to his left hand and began a long series of *naturales* so perfectly connected they seemed to be choreographed. He appeared to have the animal on a string, so gracefully did he draw him through the dangerous left-handed passes. At the end of the series, before he would go to the fence to change his light aluminum sword for a real killing sword, he prepared a final, ultimately exciting *forzado de pecho*. He left the *muleta* almost as it had ended in the last *natural* and turned his eyes to the crowd. "C'mon, Fregador," he whispered, "this is the next to the last one."

The horn pierced his buttock. Impaled, he was lifted into the air, spinning on the horn as it ripped through his flesh. Then Fregador let him fall. Bloody, spread on the sand, he looked up at the bull that prepared to drive its horns into his belly. "Fregador," he said, "you lied to me."

"Pigdog of a Jew," said Fregador. A horn punctured El Sol's belly.

El Sol looked up into the steely blue eyes of the bull as it withdrew the bloody horn and prepared to gore him again. "Oh, God," he said, recognizing the face.

A *peon* grabbed the bull's tail, trying to turn its attention away from the bleeding matador. "Yes," said Fregador, "you are correct. I vos not burned to death in zat bunker in Berlin."

El Sol went into shock.

15. A CRITICAL EXPLORATION OF THE ARTIST

At the Clínica del Perpetuo Dolor, Dr. Ignacio Nariz, the famous bullfight surgeon known to his admirers as "Manos de Plomo," prepared to operate. He put on his surgical gown, scrubbed carefully, had a light lunch of *refritos* and chicken tacos, washed it down with a bottle of Dos X, and stepped into the operating room. Chichi, the head surgical nurse, handed him a set of X rays. Dr. Nariz studied them for several moments, belching with great gravity. "An interesting wound," he said, "like crossed Z's. Six trajectories in the belly and five in the buttock. How much anesthetic are you giving him?"

"Two liters."

"Better make it two and a half," he said, moving over to the operating table to examine the intravenous feeding of the anesthetic. He licked his lips, turning the bottle slightly to read the label. "*Añejo* would be better, but this will do."

El Sol groaned softly when the doctor removed the corn cobs that had been inserted into his wound to stop the bleeding.

2

In another wing of the clinic, under a great mural depicting medicine as practiced by the Aztecs, Guero allowed Panzona to touch the bandages that covered his scalp and part of his face. "You are a brave man," she said. "We are all very proud of your wound."

"Am I on the critical list?"

"Yes," she lied. "Very critical. I can only stay a little while; the nurse said so."

Guero pushed down the covers on the side of the bed nearest her. "Take off your clothes," he said, "and get into bed with me. It could be our last time."

She began to cry. "*Querido,*" she said, "it is too dangerous. You might die from it."

Guero patted her hand. "You speak in ignorance. It is because you have not read that a man dies a little bit every time anyway."

"You are sure?" she said. "The doctors told me you should rest very quietly. We should listen to them, *querido*; they are men of science."

"Philosophy is greater than science," he said. "Take off your clothes."

3

A crowd began to gather in the lobby of the Clínica del Perpetuo Dolor immediately after the last bull was killed in the Plaza Freg. General Sanchez-Villa, accompanied by Suitcase Morales and Culo Mente the gambler, was the first to arrive. They went to the reception desk to inquire about El Sol's health. "Very grave," the girl at the desk told them.

"Thank you," said Suitcase, shaking her hand warmly and removing her wedding ring. He turned to the general. "You are a genius." The general smiled.

Culo, who had lost most of his left ear in a brawl several years before and had some experience with surgery because of that accident and the removal of his appendix in a more recent altercation, touched the nurse's naked hand. "Can I help? Maybe he needs blood. Something."

The general became apoplectic. He slammed his fist on the reception desk. "No. No, Culo. It is not the act of a sportsman. If you give one drop of blood, if you do anything to save his life, the bet is off."

"It's not a question of the bet," said Culo, explaining rather than arguing. "The man is dying. I have to help him."

"Morality," the general said, becoming less agitated, his eyes narrowing in concentration. "It is a question of morality: you took my money, you said he would live; it was a bet between gentlemen. For you to do one thing to help him now would be immoral, a sin."

Culo crossed himself, spent a moment in religious meditation, crossed himself again, then answered, "You are right, My General, it would be a mortal sin."

The general rubbed Culo's good ear affectionately. "You were guided in your decision by Christ, the greatest sportsman of all."

In a few minutes the lobby became crowded with El Sol's friends and enemies. The last to arrive was Irving Mitch, who had stopped by his hotel to pick up a tape recorder. He waited quietly in a corner, sucking on a cigar, until word leaked out from the operating room that El Sol was near death, then he turned on his machine and interviewed everyone in the room who had known the torero. He asked them all the same question: "The kid's had it, it looks like. You knew him pretty well. What would you say about him, like if, God forbid, he doesn't pull through, how would you write his obit?"

He recorded these answers:

General Sanchez-Villa: "I gave him every chance. I warned him. But you must understand, an impresario can only give opportunity; we do not control fate. When a boy has such a desire to be a matador, there is danger—he is going to take chances. This boy had courage, he worked very hard in training, but he had no natural talent. Death was inevitable. I am always sad when a torero is killed in the ring, but in the case of this fine American boy, I am more deeply sad than usual, for he was my friend and I loved him. I owe him much."

Delia Monroe: "He was a sweet boy, who had a streak of anarchy in him that may have cost him his life. Yes, he was still a boy, unsophisticated and sweet. He made mistakes, of course, social errors that would have been unforgivable in anyone less talented. Artists, like El Sol, give so much. As my father says, though, we must learn to accept their generosity and take whatever we can from them without remorse."

Armero II: "He was murdered. That is the only word for it. The general killed him. I warned him. I told him about men like Sanchez-Villa. I told him the difference between the good death and the early death. Who knows why he wouldn't listen to me? There is something inside a man who wants to fight bulls that has no name. It is a kind of madness. The ones who have it and survive become artists, great artists, like me. The ones who do not have it are poor suicides. He was a good boy, but he had no luck. He had a great resistance to disease."

Hijo de Quien: "He was the greatest, most brave, graceful and beautiful North American matador I have ever met. He was a victim of the bloodsucker; I have seen it before. We pray for the conversion of his soul in heaven."

Doris Miller: "I am going to sit *shiva* for him. I'll spend the next eight days sitting on an orange crate by the television set in deepest communion with the gods who made this happen. He was a nice boy, with such a good heart. Somebody should mourn him. I couldn't give him what he wanted when he was alive, but maybe I can do it now. Experiences like this change a girl, you know. He always called me Princess. I didn't deserve it."

Lala: "I do not believe in hypocrisy. Death does not

give a man grace. This Mr. Feldman, or El Sol as he chose to call himself, was an amateur. Had he not been a North American, I doubt he would ever have appeared in a major plaza. Mark me, however, I do not mean to denigrate his desire to be a torero—he had the spirit of an artist. His performance was quite another matter. He walked like a hooked fish. His work with the cape and *muleta* was all cobblestones and potholes. Really, he lacked silk in his sinew and in his soul. He would never have been successful as a torero; his death is not regrettable for that reason, but for the fact only that he was a human being who died before his time and in a violent way. No, I should say that he died in the very beginning of his suffering. If I were pressed to give a reason for the course of his life, I would have to say that it was the repression of his homosexual instincts. That is not unusual in artists who fail, you know. The life and death of Sol Feldman is by no means unique. I tried to advise him as I have advised so many others, but he could not control certain of his defense mechanisms. He tended to be rude in the face of the inescapable truths of the artistic life."

Consequencias: "I think he would have been one of the greatest toreros if he had seasoned his food properly."

Bisco refused to speak into the microphone. "I do not believe he is dead," he told Mitch, "and you better get out of here with that machine and this talk about him being dead or I'll tear you in half. Parasite! I'll shove that cigar right up your nose. You think I'd take a short position on my friend?"

Adolph "Nagadoches" North: "The trouble with your kind of writing is that you don't go beyond the surface of things. You don't have the intelligence to see into the real meanings, baby. Maybe it's the fact that so many of you are Jewish. Now, I admire the musical abilities of Jews; they're the greatest of all the violinists, but when it comes to understanding the society we live in, that's a horse of another color. We blacks are more involved in the now of it all, so we can be more thoroughly alienated. You can see what that means in terms of the requisites for understanding. And then, of course, we're funny, which is something you would like to be, but you can't because of this lack of involvement and alienation I was talking about. Death is a black phenomenon. Do you see what I mean, Mr. Goldberg?"

Suitcase Morales: "I owe him a ballpoint pen. I also owe him a typewriter, a record player, a radio, two cameras, three sets of cufflinks, the price of a watch three times, a keychain, two tiepins, a pair of binoculars, two regular pens and a false tooth."

Mitch even carried his tape recorder to Guero's room, where the *banderillero* was still in bed with his wife. Guero pushed Panzona to one side while he spoke with Mitch. For a moment after the writer finished his explanation of the tape recordings and the imminent death of El Sol, the *banderillero* cried openly. Then, composing himself, he beckoned to Mitch to bring the microphone closer. "Xtlanzliltlaque, the great Maya philosopher, once said that to die you must have lived. What can I, a poor *peon*, add to such profundity?" He was quiet for several moments; the corners of his mouth melted in despair. "Well, perhaps there is one thing I can add," he said. "I heard it once at a Masonic Hall lecture. You would not know the man who said it; he's not famous in your country. Here, he is known as The Railroad Track because his thoughts are so straight. It was he who said that the death of a friend is like sundown on a potato." He turned away from the microphone to embrace Panzona. They wept together.

"Wait a minute," Mitch said. "That's garbage. It doesn't make any sense."

Guero left off embracing his wife for a moment,

turning his watery eyes to the famous writer. "My oldest daughter," he said, with disgust showing in his voice and in the curl of his mouth, "is a Mexican psychotherapist. She has intimate knowledge of many men like you, Señor Mitch. I think what she says about you is true. You believe life is a flower."

4

Dr. Nariz finished stitching up the wound in El Sol's buttock and rolled him over onto his back. He asked for a swab and a probe. Chichi pressed them into his hand, then lifted them out again. "I think it's too late," she said; "he's not breathing."

The doctor took a mirror from the instrument tray and placed it close to El Sol's lips. When he took it away, there was no moisture condensed on the glass. "Dead," he said.

16. THE RESURRECTION OF
SOL FELDMAN

Chichi began to cry. "What is it?" the doctor asked her. "Why are you crying? You didn't know him."

"It's a cumulative effect. We lose so many."

Dr. Nariz shrugged. "We give them the best medical science can offer, what else can we do? If you want, you can call in the *curandero*."

Chichi hurried out of the operating room to fetch Sucio Malcontento, the *curandero*, who also worked as a janitor in the abortion wing of the clinic. The old man was curing a wart on a retired prostitute's tongue when she found him. As soon as Chichi explained that it was a matter of life and death, he put the snake's eyes and the toad tongue into his pocket and scurried off to the operating room, his arthritic knuckles brushing the floor with every step.

Sucio examined the patient quickly, then announced his diagnosis: "The man has died of sterility."

"Impossible," said Dr. Nariz. He took a meat cleaver from the instrument tray. "We'll do an autopsy."

"If you whack off the top of his head or something, I can't save his life," said Sucio.

"But if I don't whack off the top of his head, how will we know what killed him?"

Sucio made a wart appear on the end of his nose to focus the doctor's attention on him. "My dear colleague," he said, "if you whack off the top of this man's head, we will know exactly what killed him. Now, calm yourself, and let me explain to you why he no longer breathes. You must understand the body. It is like a pendulum. Watch my hand." He moved his hand up and back in front of the doctor's face. "That is the movement of a pendulum, right?"

"Yes."

"How does it go?"

"From left to right," the doctor answered.

"And what would happen if the pendulum could not swing past the center, but could only go from right to center?"

"It would stop."

"Aha!" said the *curandero*, jumping onto a chair, putting his eyes on a level with those of the doctor, "now you see why he has stopped breathing."

"No," said the doctor, looking directly into the *curandero*'s eyes, "and you have incipient glaucoma."

"Never mind that," said Sucio; "it is easily cured with eagle dung. We must think of this man who is not breathing. Back to the body. Now, there are two kinds of cells, good cells and bad cells. The good cells are the white corpuscles and the bad cells are the germs, right?"

"Yes, yes," said the doctor, still peering into Sucio's eyes, "but I think you are having a stroke. If you'll wait a minute, I'll get my ophthalmoscope."

"Don't worry about the living; let us tend to the dead," said Sucio. "Think now, Doctor, the body is sometimes well and sometimes sick. What causes it to be sick?"

"Germs."

"And when the germs are defeated by the white cells, the body becomes well again?"

"More or less."

"Then the body is like a pendulum, swinging from sickness to health." The doctor agreed, and Sucio quickly followed with, "So then by removing the germs from the room by sterilizing it, you stop the pendulum in the middle and let it swing only one way, right?"

Dr. Nariz looked blank. He was thinking. Suddenly, he threw the meat cleaver at the frosted-glass window beside him, smashing the window. "Filth," he shouted, "bring filth." Chichi and the other nurses began to spit and urinate on the floor and walls. "No," he cried, "bring real filth. Hurry, a life depends on it."

Sucio made a second nose grow on his cheek to attract the doctor's attention. "Listen to me," he said. "It's too late for that. First, we must wind the clock before we start the pendulum swinging again. Bring me one juicy *jalapeño* and three pubic hairs from a fertile woman."

Dr. Nariz gave him one of the peppers left over from his lunch, and when Chichi came back into the room carrying the contents of a grease trap in the hollow of her skirt, he told her to allow the *curandero* to pluck three of her pubic hairs. Sucio jumped down from the chair, scurried over to Chichi and reached under her skirt.

"Ouch! Ayii! Aaayiii! Ooooh!" At the last sound the doctor smacked the *curandero* on the back and told him, "Remember? The dead before the living."

The *curandero* made an ugly face at the doctor and uttered a curse in Toltec which caused the doctor's penis to become parallel to his pelvis, then he jumped up onto the operating table. He straddled the dead torero, sat on his chest and grabbed his nose. With his other hand, he got a firm grip on El Sol's chin, and, by lifting the nose up and pulling the chin down, he forced his mouth open. "Chichi," he said, "squeeze the juice of the *jalapeño* into his mouth." While the juice ran into El Sol's mouth, Sucio chanted loudly in Toltec.

"The chile is dry," said Chichi after several minutes. Sucio thanked her, and began to bounce up and down on the torero's chest. "We must stir up the corpse," he said. The *curandero* counted to one hundred and three in Toltec, then climbed off the torero and onto a chair near the operating table. He leaned over the table to tickle El Sol's nose with the three hairs.

The corpse inhaled. "He lives!" the nurses screamed. "The gringo lives!"

El Sol sniffed at the hairs several times, then stuck out his tongue. "You see," said Sucio, "a gringo dies and is resurrected a Latin."

17. ART IS NOT FOR THE WEARY
OR THE SIX-LEGGED

Doris Miller was tired. The weight of her gigantic breasts pulled her shoulders down and forward over her lap, causing a mean ache in her back. She took two small telescoping stands out of her purse, opened them and placed them on her knees. Carefully, she laid a breast atop each of the stands. Victorious over the plague of gravity, she was able to lean back in the chair and feel comfortable.

There was only one dim light in the lobby of the Clínica del Perpetuo Dolor. The receptionist had left hours before. The friends and enemies of El Sol too had gone. Many had left immediately after the announcement of his death. The weepers remained until the announcement of his resurrection, when all but the few who could also weep for joy had gone. Bisco and Armero were the last to leave. They had wanted to speak to the torero before going, but Armero had complained that he did not like to wander in the streets in the darkness and nagged Bisco into escorting him to the alley where he usually slept. Doris had been alone in the lobby for more than an hour.

Her toes and the farthest tips of her breasts had grown cold with night and waiting when a nurse at last appeared and whispered, "He is awake now. I can take you to him." Doris closed the breast rests and slipped them back into her purse. She arose slowly. Her knees creaked. As she followed the nurse down the long corridors leading to El Sol's room, she straightened a drooping eyelash and powdered the tiny scars of plastic surgery on her ears and nose.

The torero was sitting up in bed when she entered. "Thank God," she said, rushing to embrace him and nearly falling over the uncovered garbage cans that had been brought into the room to maintain the essential life balances. They kissed with friendly passion. "How did it feel to be dead?" she asked him.

"I don't know; I was asleep when it happened."

"Poor thing," she said, leaning over him, resting her breasts on his shoulders, "you must be very weak."

"No, I feel fine," he told her. "In fact, if you didn't have that trouble with your stomach . . ."

"Try me." She stepped back from the bed and did a few flamenco steps. The garbage cans rattled and the bed shook. He applauded softly and asked her to make a little less noise since it was after midnight. She pouted for a moment, then changed her mind and disrobed with a willing smile. He asked if she wanted him to put out the light. "Please don't," she answered. "I went to more trouble than you'll ever know to get a figure like this; I like to show it off. That's why I could never be happy with a nearsighted man; he could never appreciate my nose and my nipples at the same time. And they're the things that came most dear."

They were gentle, mindful of his wounds. "How's your stomach?" he said.

"Fine," she said.

"It doesn't bother you anymore?"

"No."

"Since when?"

"Armero," she said.

"You and Armero?"

"Uh huh."

"Oh, God," he said, "I've got syphilis."

He tried to roll away from her, but she held on to him. "Don't be afraid. Syphilis is good for you."

"Let go," he said, wrenching himself free of her. A stitch broke and blood began to ooze from the crossed Z's on his belly. "Now look what you've done," he said, "you and that damned Armero."

"But syphilis is good for you. It brings peace of mind to everyone, and it prolongs the life of bullfighters. Armero explained it to me."

El Sol pinched his wound together to stop the bleeding. "Armero is a tired, old man. Maybe syphilis is good for him. He's had his time. He's too tired to be an artist, but I'm not. I don't want to be diseased. Not yet."

Doris backed off the bed. She had difficulty standing up because of the weight of her breasts. "Well," she said, "the course of my life is clear; you can do what you want. I don't have to worry about bad marriages or unhappy children or even the atomic bomb. I know everything that's going to happen to me. I'm free of anxiety. And I owe it all to syphilis."

He threw the bedpan at her. Stumbling through the garbage cans, she grabbed her clothes and backed out of the room. "I hope you get cured!" she screamed. Then, with quiet vindictiveness, she added, "I pray that you'll always enjoy the best of health."

The nurse closed the wound with a clothespin, explaining that the doctor would be back in the morning to replace the broken stitches. El Sol lay on his side, resting his weight on his good cheek, and had fantasies about penicillin shots. After a long time, he turned out the light and tried to sleep. He was just drifting off when a loud rasping noise awakened him. Sam was standing on the wall next to his bed. "Ah," he said, "I've been expecting you. I suppose you've come to gloat over my wounds."

Double rasp.

"Well, that's very compassionate of you. Would it please you to know that I've got syphilis, too?"

Rasp.

"I'll be getting penicillin in the morning. How does that strike you?"

Silence.

"You'd rather see me blind and stupid than a bull-fighter, wouldn't you?"

Rasp.

"So you'll do anything you can to keep me from being a bullfighter? You know what's best."

Rasp.

"Well, maybe you're just mad because you can't be a bullfighter? Maybe it isn't for guys with six legs?"

Double rasp.

"The tough guys always win, don't they? I guess a human slob like me doesn't have a chance against you."

Emphatic rasp.

El Sol lay quietly, watching Sam. The cockroach pranced on five legs. With the other leg he hid his eyes in mock shame over his easy victory. The torero nodded his head, sadly understanding. Then he shouted, "Nurse, there's a cockroach in my room! Nurse! Nurse!" Sam ran. Up the wall and down, in circles and squares. He ran until the stickiness gave out on his feet and he tumbled to the floor. Then he ran around the floor, bumping into baseboards and bedposts, his feet stumbling over each other.

El Sol watched him and laughed. He kept on laughing until the crossed Z's faded from his belly and his torn buttock became whole again. He felt a stirring in his bowels. He would be in the plaza again on Sunday. No one could stop him now, not even Lala or the general. He had been the witness of his own miracle; he was an artist.

GLOSSARY

Aguantar—to hold your ground.

Añejo—aged tequila.

Ayudado—a fake sword of wood or aluminum used in place of the heavy killing sword during the *faena*.

Banderillero—one who places *banderillas*, the barbed sticks used to "encourage" the bull and sometimes to alter the manner of his charge.

Bisco—cockeyed.

Burladero—escape hatch through which bullfighters run, thus mocking the bull.

Caca caliente—hot poo poo.

Capote—a large cape of raw silk, magenta on one side and yellow on the other. *Toreros* are said to earn *olé's* with the *capote*, ears with the *muleta*, and money with the sword.

Carnitas—small pieces of barbecued pork, a great delicacy.

Cartel—bill, poster.

Chapo—Shorty.

Clínica de Poco Socorro—Clinic of Little Mercy.

Clínica del Perpetuo Dolor—Clinic of the Perpetual Pain.

Cochino—pig.

Conejo—rabbit.

Corrida—a bullfight; literally, the running (of the bulls).

Costillas—ribs, chops.

Cruz Roja—Red Cross.

Cuadrilla—bullfighter's entourage.

Culo Mente—Anus Mind.

Curandero—witchdoctor.

Derechazo—classic pass with the *muleta* held in the right hand.

Despreciado—despised, scorned.

Divino—divine one.

Dr. Ignacio Nariz—Dr. Ignatz Nose.

El Día de los Malcriados—The Day of the Ill-bred.

El Macho—The Virile One.

El Número Uno—the number one, the best.

Ejido—a communal farm.

Faena—the third act of the bullfight, leading to the kill.

Feo—Ugly.

Feria—a fair.

Forzado de pecho—the pass most often used to complete a series of *naturales,* in which the *muleta* is brought from aft to fore at chest level.

Fregador—one who wipes out or washes up others.

Gitano Fregado—Washed-up Gypsy.

Guero—Blondie.

Guitarrón—a big guitar.

Hijo de Quien—Son of Whom.

Hotel Cojon—Hotel Testicle.

Huaraches—Florsheim de Mexico.

Huevos—eggs; slang, testicles.

Jalapeño—a formidable green chile pepper.

La Gachupina—The Spic.

La Tortillera—one who makes tortillas; slang, lesbian.

Malagueña Miedosa—The Cowardly Lady from Málaga.

Mamarracho—sucker.

Manos de Plomo—Hands of Lead.

Matacoño—Rapist.

Menudo—a soup of tripe.

Miedo—fear.

M.M.—Moneda Mexicana—Mexican currency (12½ pesos to the dollar).

Monosabios—wise monkeys.

Montera—a hat with ears.

Morrillo—the bull's tossing muscle.

Muleta—a small cape of red serge, folded over a stick.

Nalga de Tijuana—rump steak in hot sauce.

Naturales—classic passes with the *muleta* held in the left hand.

Novale Verga—Unworthy of Coitus.

Novillero—one who fights small bulls (*novillos*); a young bullfighter, like a young American writer, usually less than fifty years old.

Oye—listen.

Palomo—Dove.

Panzona—Big Belly, Pregnant.

Paso Doble—the Spanish two-step, not akin to the Aztec two-step.

Peon de confianza—a bullfighter's trusted *peon*.

Pimienta—Pepper.

Pollo Asado—barbecued chicken.

Querido—dear.

Ratón—Mouse.
Refritos—*frijoles* twice blessed.

Sr. Riendo of Inhumaciones Riendos—Mr. Laughing of Laughing Burials.
Sincero—Sincere.
Sorteo—drawing of lots for the bulls.
Suave—Smoothie.
Sucio Malcontento—Filthy Malcontent.

Tauromaquia—the art of bullfighting (a definition of art is not offered).
Tío Pedo—Uncle Fart.

Vara—picador's pole.
Veneno—Poison.
Verguenza—shame.
Veronica—classic pass with the *capote*.

A NOVEL

7TH AVE.

"A novel of sex and ambition. . . . Everybody is
going to be reading SEVENTH AVENUE"
—*Washington Star*

SEVENTH AVENUE
by Norman Bogner

*From showroom to bedroom, a bold novel about
New York's glittering fashion world.*

"Norman Bogner has created characters who are real,
capable of being loved, hated, pitied, and above all, believed. His work is about hunger and passion, sex and love,
hatred and revenge, pity and disgust, dissipation and
nobility. It is life."
—*Nashville Banner*

"The scorching success of Jay Blackman . . . ripping his
way from a two-bit basement peddling rags to become a
multimillionaire operator . . . enormous, penetrating and
perceptive"
—*Portland Sunday Telegram*

"A narrative gift . . . a sure hand with character . . . con-
vincing . . . impressive"
—*Saturday Review Syndicate*

A DELL BOOK 95¢

If you cannot obtain copies of this title at your local bookseller, just send
the price (plus 10c per copy for handling and postage) to Dell Books, Box
2291, Grand Central Post Office, New York, N.Y. 10017. No postage or handling
charge is required on any order of five or more books.

*It had to be written as fiction—
her story is that hot!*

The
Symbol

by Alvah Bessie

Possibly no other actress gave more of herself
on the screen—and off the screen—than the subject of this blistering biographical novel.   On
the screen she could generate heat faster than
the sun.   Her personal life, tragic and chaotic,
was even more sensational.   The novel moves
from this great beauty's early childhood to her
days as a photographer's model and bit player.
It tells of her phenomenal rise in Hollywood,
her disastrous love affairs and marriages, her
growing dependence on alcohol and sleeping
pills, and finally her tragic suicide.

A DELL BOOK   95c

A sensational
novel about a
non-stop weekend
of emotional
striptease, a radical
new kind of
group therapy!

The
Lemon
Eaters

by Jerry Sohl

*They came together for a weekend in a California motel—twelve very
different people. Plus the psychologist who was supposed to lead them.
Ahead lay the most shattering hours of their lives. Before the weekend
was over, a marriage would be destroyed and another saved, love
consummated and love betrayed, hatred unleashed and the most intimate human secrets laid bare. Before it was over, something drastic
would happen to each man and woman there.*

A DELL BOOK 95c

JAMES JONES

sensational new bestseller

"His best since FROM HERE TO ETERNITY"
—Saturday Review

GO TO THE WIDOW-MAKER

An epic story of one man's search for true courage and manliness in terms of his relationships with a former mistress who seeks to possess him; a magnificent young woman who loves him, and a brute of a man whose world of physical violence and courage tempts him toward a disastrous self-betrayal.

"A man's book that many women will love."
—*Life Magazine*

"A provocative contribution to contemporary American culture ... total candor, describing in detail the virtuoso sexual performance of his characters."
—*Saturday Review*

A DELL BOOK $1.25